SOUTHERLY

First published by Charco Press 2017
Second expanded edition by Charco Press 2023
Charco Press Ltd., Office 59, 44–46 Morningside Road, Edinburgh EH10 4BF

This book was originally published in Spanish by Eterna Cadencia
(Argentina) under the title *Villa del Parque*.

Work published with funding from the 'Sur' Translation Support Program
of the Ministry of Foreign Affairs and Worship of Argentina / Obra
editada en el marco del Programa 'Sur' de Apoyo a las Traducciones del
Ministerio de Relaciones Exteriores y Culto de la República Argentina.

A CIP catalogue record for this book is available from the British Library.

ISBN: 9781913867577
e-book: 9781913867584

www.charcopress.com

Edited by Fionn Petch
Cover design by Pablo Font
Typeset by Laura Jones
Proofread by Fiona Mackintosh

2 4 6 8 10 9 7 5 3 1

Jorge Consiglio

SOUTHERLY

Translated by
Cherilyn Elston & Carolina Orloff

CHARCO PRESS

CONTENTS

SOUTHERLY

In June 1912 a merchant ship was delayed entering Buenos Aires. During the hours they were kept waiting, the passengers – all on deck – gazed ashore in search of clues about what the future held. They saw cranes, silos, a group of freezing people (the temperature was -2°C) and the serrated outline of a tower. Everything else was shrouded in fog. The chaotic disembarkation represented the conclusion of one chapter of their lives. Yet the minds of the new arrivals were already fixed on the next one. They believed that life was just beginning, that they were starting anew. A young man – tall, stocky and redheaded – broke away from the crowd and strode across the port as if he knew where he was going, heading towards the streets of the city centre. His name was Czcibor Zakowicz. He carried a cardboard suitcase and was wearing a duffel coat. In his pocket was a piece of paper with a name and an address on it. A distant relative, the cousin of a cousin, was expecting him and would put him up and feed him. Zakowicz would do the rest. He found work at a cabinetmaker's and, in a short time, discovered his relationship with wood was not that of a craftsman. He was organised and successful. He set up a workshop in the Flores quarter and found a talent for inventing fanciful myths. He combined work with tradition and sacrifice.

After he turned forty-five, his eyebrow hair began to grow. It became a wild, unkempt thicket that covered the ridge of his brow, curving downwards into his eye sockets until it brushed his eyelids. In the first few years, Czcibor Zakowicz tried to domesticate his brows. He trimmed them every week, more out of embarrassment than vanity. However, it is common knowledge that laziness tends to get the better of even the most determined. Eventually, Zakowicz became resigned to his appearance, and something changed in the look in his eyes.

The same thing happened to one of his grandchildren, when he turned fifty. He inherited his grandfather's overflowing eyebrows, and suffered similar embarrassment until he in turn conceded defeat. He also inherited his grandfather's sense of urgency, which had made him ambitious in his career. He was an estate agent. In keeping with family tradition – a romantic absurdity – they called him Anatol, and that is how his name was recorded on his birth certificate. He, a skilful operator, took advantage of the exoticism of his name – not his surname but his first name – and turned it into a brand. It was the perfect combination of something both straightforward and unusual, two decisive factors when it comes to selling properties in fashionable neighbourhoods. Anatol, married to a very light-skinned woman, understands like no other the secret of his era, its fickle essence. His company's logo, for example, is adapted from a nineteenth-century Danish ex libris with text in the Garamond typeface. The efficacy of maximising artifice, an aesthetics of defiance, of bravado. All coming together as one great, effective masquerade. Nothing is concealed from the client, not even their own stupidity.

Anatol's last great move was to relocate his office to the Bencich building on Diagonal Sur. The spot he reserved for his desk is on the ninth floor. It is a spacious room, with an enormous painting as its only adornment. There is something paradoxical about the canvas: at first glance, the observer is moved by the stillness of the image, yet at the same time by its furious dynamism. The meaning of each stroke is drawn from a point located in infinity. It depicts the face of a man who is neither young nor old, with a beard and a blank expression. This work of art is another of Anatol's expensive whims. It is a copy of a daguerreotype left to him by his grandfather Czcibor. It was painted by a certain Zorroaquín, one of the highest-paid contemporary artists.

It has to be said that the new office changed Anatol's behaviour. It impaired something that has always concerned him and that he happens to call productivity. The view from his office is irresistible. He spends all his time gazing at the domes of the surrounding buildings: the neo-colonial dome of the Boston Bank, the geometric one of La Equitativa de Plata, the neoclassical dome of the other Bencich building; to the south, the tower of the City Legislature building and, to the west, the side of the Barolo Palace and the National Congress. He is also fascinated by the vast stretch of river that can be glimpsed behind the Plaza de Mayo. There is yet another distraction for Anatol in this building. His name is von Hefty. He is a lawyer and has his office on the eighth floor. His father, a Hungarian, was a despotic Protestant pastor. The second time they took the lift together, Anatol and von Hefty only exchanged a brief glance, but they were sure they were going to get along. The third time they spoke about a shared passion: chess. They study the moves made by the world's best players in historic matches. They compare and discuss them. Currently they're studying a move from 1866 when the Austrian Steinitz defeated Andersson. Anatol has it on his iPad and he can't stop analysing it. At times he decodes, or thinks he has decoded, the logic behind Steinitz's move, his system, and he feels that he is Steinitz, as if a more intelligent man inhabited his mind and the flow of ideas of each – host and visitor – ran parallel up to a certain point where they fused and became one. When this happens he is overwhelmed by terror and a strange euphoria. He stands up, walks to the window and takes several breaths. He then calls his wife and tells her what has just happened. Sometimes, he drinks green tea to calm himself down. Right now, he's in that state of agitated excitement but, as the move he has just understood ends in checkmate, he doesn't do what he normally does; instead he goes downstairs to share his discovery with von Hefty. It's just one floor and Anatol wants to cover the distance in an instant. He flies down the stairs with the iPad in his hand. All of a sudden, the very same euphoria that is propelling him forwards clouds his vision, without warning or preamble. He can't see a thing. He tries to feel his way down the steps and falls headlong, coming to a standstill against a door. Wounded in body and spirit, he has only one thought before losing consciousness. He's sure it's the end.

He wakes up in a clinic on Calle San Martín de Tours. The first thing he sees is his wife, Iris, tall and elegant, talking to a priest. The clergyman's body language conveys the complexity of the issue they are discussing. Anatol's lips are dry, he's dying of thirst; but he waits a while before asking for water. The liquid runs down his oesophagus and Anatol realises his pain threshold is light years away from where he thought it was. Then, as if he were a child, he covers his face with his hands and cries. The last time he did this he was twelve years old.

His recovery is so slow that weeks go by before any improvement is noted. According to the doctors this is progress. They explain to Anatol that he nearly died. This fact comes in handy to keep him quiet: they can't stand his moaning. They express their exasperation behind his back. Iris indifferently monitors her husband's convalescence during her afternoon visits. The rest of the day the patient remains alone. Anatol chats to the nurses – one of them talks about trivial things: his morning mate ritual – and he observes how the room changes with the passing hours. At night clonazepam puts him to sleep, but he has a recurring dream he can't get out of his mind. It is an image: a man dressed in the style of the 1950s, who is at once himself and another, is stroking an enormous cat in a public place. The third time he has this dream he realises they are in a café on Calle Brazil. The clarity of the image surprises him. It all ends the morning he is discharged. The insistent dream vanishes, together with the blessing of easy sleep. Anatol makes an effort to get back to normal but when he imagines his daily life he is moved to tears. He feels like he doesn't have the strength to go on.

Anatol resumes normal activity bit by bit. For breakfast he has fruit, orange juice, something sweet. For lunch, well-done veal. He avoids staying up late and being out in the cold. He returns to work and his chats with von Hefty, who has become a man of few words, almost abrupt, perhaps because he feels guilty about his friend's accident.

It's Wednesday afternoon and Anatol gets a call from his wife. She suggests they do something fun: a weekend trip to the coast. She says it's just what they need, there's no better cure than being by the sea. Anatol can't really face the journey but he hopes it will ease the bitterness he feels. Since the accident, he notices that reality has become distorted. Things seem flimsier. The world is now light, airy. It can disappear, alter its state or form.

Iris has taken the car, a white Kia, to the garage for a service. She has packed two small bags and bought a fruit loaf for the journey. It's Friday, six in the morning. They drive south down Calle Junín. Anatol is at the wheel. He is freshly shaven; he smells of 212 by Carolina Herrera. He takes pleasure in his wife's deep voice, the tactility of the steering wheel and the intimacy of the car interior. The city is deserted. A cool breeze shakes the tree branches and drags the fallen leaves towards the storm drains. A bus moves along Avenida Córdoba. It seems to be alone, abandoned; a column of black smoke rises from the exhaust. Further ahead a pack of dogs sniff the rubbish bins; a few metres away, on the same block, a caretaker rolls up an endless hose. Sounds are muffled and infrequent.

The Kia is a soundproof capsule. It glides along, barely touching the ground, taking on an existence of its own. On the corner of Corrientes it stops at a traffic light. A nondescript man with a bag over his shoulder crosses the road. He is looking down at the ground. He is on his way to or from work. As he steps onto the pavement, the traffic light turns green. The car starts moving.

Everything flows: the city blocks rush by with a pleasant sense of vertigo. The perfect excuse to get lost in details, a silent stage-set, the ideal context for thinking about something else. Anatol and his wife are overcome by an unaccustomed sense of peace. They enter a limbo of calm. Their habitual decorum loosens. It's been years since they've felt like this, so relaxed. This is why when they cross Rivadavia and a poorly-executed manoeuvre – a lane change, a distraction, a mistake – puts them in danger, the shock makes their blood run cold. Iris doesn't understand what is happening; Anatol even less so. He grips the steering wheel, his eyes wide open. He assumes he's done nothing wrong so is surprised, and immediately enraged, when he hears someone insulting him from a VW estate. It's a young man, under forty. He's travelling with a heavily made-up, loud-mouthed woman. Anatol's fuse is short: he returns the aggression. Now they're both raring to go. They lower their windows. They make threatening gestures. They wave their fists in the air. They scream at the top of their lungs. The street is a wasteland, which only multiplies the absurdity of the situation. All of a sudden, the other driver reaches boiling point. He swerves violently and blocks the Kia's path. Anatol could reverse, put the car into first gear and continue on his way – after all he is still in convalescence – but he doesn't react. He sits and waits for the guy to get out of his car. He watches him walk towards the Kia. He thinks he recognises the other driver. He realises he's the spitting image of one of the nurses in the hospital. Anatol inhales deeply through his nose. His rival is stocky, square-built, with a face like a spade. He sways from side to side in an exaggerated fashion, as if he were drunk, and this exaggeration is a savage form of mockery. He is inviting Anatol to fight. For a few seconds the world stands still; yet this is not the paralysis of indecision nor the good sense of fear. The moment has come. Anatol glances sideways at his wife. He opens the car door and, as his foot searches for the ground, it dawns on him that the battle he is about to fight is as necessary as it is senseless.

CORRESPONDENCE

What can be seen in the blink of an eye
if not the fleeting nature of sight?
Alberto Szpunberg

When I first came to Buenos Aires, Zulema, the woman who brought me up, wouldn't hear anything about me living alone. 'You're so absent-minded, they'd eat you alive in two weeks,' she said in her husky voice. When I think about her, the same image always comes to mind. I see her in the half-light of the kitchen. She's standing, straight as a rod. Her eyes are two bugs. She hardly blinks. Her lips are slightly parted. In her right hand is a fly swatter; a cloth hangs from her left. She waits. She knows the fly's flight range is limited. When it comes to a standstill, she'll deliver the blow. She'll immediately wipe away any traces. That's the idea. Such a mission requires the greatest care, all her attention. That's Zulema, with her glass of orange liqueur, her herbal tea, her lacquered hairstyle, her determination, which is like saying her strategies for survival. They deserve respect. The survival strategies, I mean. You've got to be on the ball. I'm sure she's just the same today.

★

I live with my uncle Mundo and his ten-year-old daughter on the sixth floor of a building on Carlos Calvo. Let me explain: I had only ever seen my uncle and Angela, his daughter, in photos before coming here. Back in the village there was a lot of talk about them, particularly him: about his divorce, how brave he was to have taken responsibility for the child, and his prestigious job as a cardiologist at the Hospital Italiano.

The first time I saw him I was struck dumb. He was only slightly taller than I was. I had imagined him to be huge: in the photos he looked like a giant. There is one photo I remember in particular: Mundo is descending a staircase – I found out later that this was in the Hospital de Clínicas – with a colleague. It was a bright, sunny day. Both were wearing scrubs. The photographer was standing at the foot of the stairs, on the pavement. It looked like a natural shot. They were deep in conversation, pretending the camera wasn't there. Mundo was trying to look assertive, powerful. His hands were frozen in a gesture that encapsulated his entire surroundings: the city, the people, the traffic, the traffic lights. I thought a guy like that couldn't be less than six foot tall. These were assumptions I'd made at home in the village, the fantasies of a child. We met. He said to me: 'Hello, Mariela.' I opened my mouth but nothing came out. He repeated: 'Hello, Mariela.' I rubbed my hands and said: 'But we're the same height.' I have no idea why I said that. I heard myself say the words as if someone else had spoken for me. Then we fell silent. We looked at each other. I was waiting for a rebuke; he, I suppose, for an explanation.

★

Angela and I got on instantly. She was fascinated by me. I had just turned twenty: I took the role of older sister. She'd stroke my arms, sniff my clothes, stick her fingers into my pots of Hinds cream. Whenever we could we'd hang out and gossip. Saturday afternoons were our favourite time. She'd come to my room (which was the smallest, at the end of the corridor) with her brushes and combs. She'd spend hours doing my hair, telling me her secrets. And I would let her. I listened to her life in miniature and I sensed, I don't know why, that she was in danger. Poor little thing. I envisaged her in the middle of a suspension bridge hanging over an abyss. Frozen with fear at the drop below. Bewitched, waiting for a voice, I assume her father's, to encourage her on. Once, after eating an entire box of Lindt, she fixed her eyes on me. The chocolate had revealed something to her. She said: 'Mariela: I'm afraid of myself.' Those were her exact words: 'I'm afraid of myself.' She didn't have to say it twice. 'It's okay, sweetheart,' I said. I gave her a big hug. She was my cuddly toy, my lucky charm.

★

Ever since I moved in, Angela dropped hints that she wanted me to buy her a pet. My uncle, like all men, was sedentary, depressive. He refused to have an animal in the house. I didn't care what he thought. We shared a very small past, or no past at all. That, and my lack of experience, were my armour. One day I went to a pet shop and bought a golden hamster, a cage, a water bottle and an exercise ball. Angela jumped for joy. 'It's for you, honey,' I said. 'Give it a name.'

But the hamster lasted what hamsters last: no time at all. A week later, Angela had an allergic reaction. She came out in a rash on her neck, nose, cheeks and arms. Her eyelids swelled up. She couldn't breathe properly. We had to rush her to A&E. They injected her with corticosteroids. The doctor broke the news: 'There's a risk of oedema of the glottis.' My eyes opened wide. 'I can't believe it,' I said. He clarified: 'The glottis is an opening in the larynx. Through which air passes.' I felt like I was going to die. Everything turned blue. I steadied myself against the back of a chair. I almost fainted.

I didn't give up. A week later I bought a canary, but Angela had lost interest in animals. I was the one who became fond of the bird. I discovered the way in which birds make themselves present. How to put it. They're unpredictable. Sometimes silent, keeping an ear to the ground; at other times, frenziedly chirping. They're strange creatures. We give our canary birdseed, apple, a little carrot, but some days it won't touch its food. The vet told us it was suffering from melancholy. It only eats when it wants to.

★

I hate how dingy the flat is. I'm used to sunlight streaming through the windows. In Carlos Calvo we had to have the light on all day long. The flat is a hole in the wall. That's why it took me a while to clean the top shelf of my wardrobe. I only got round to it one Sunday a month after my arrival. I stood on a chair, opened the doors and dusted the inside. As I went to wipe the shelf with a wet cloth, I noticed some abandoned papers stuck right at the back. I brought them down.

Two legal-size envelopes. One contained a letter and some photos; the other an X-ray and a guide to playing the piano. I started with the photos. There were four. Three in black and white and one in colour in which you could make out two old ladies on a patio full of potted plants. They were sitting on plastic chairs around a table with a bottle of Coke and four glasses. They were smiling. It was summer: they were wearing sleeveless flowery smocks. The other photos were even older. The scene was an empty beach. It seemed remote. It showed a young woman, about thirty, walking beside the shore. The other two were alike: the girl was wearing jodhpurs and a black polo shirt. In the background, partly hidden by the sand dunes, was a tower. At first I thought it was a lighthouse; then I realised I was mistaken. It was the chimney of a factory or something like that.

★

I pushed aside the other documents and concentrated on the photos. I spent several weeks studying them. I was obsessed. I couldn't take my eyes off those images. Then I began working as an administrator at an estate agency and started studying at college. These two things kept me busy all day. I would leave the flat at nine in the morning and would get home at half ten at night, when I'd warm up some leftovers in the microwave, eat quickly and go straight to bed. Sometimes, I'd find my uncle slumped on the sofa watching a film. One evening, he got up, turned off the telly and made coffee. 'I'll keep you company,' he said, and sat down opposite me with the cup in his hand. It was extremely uncomfortable. I didn't know what to say and he didn't say anything. He just watched me eat. I started talking nonstop. I got really nervous. This always happens to me. I told him about my job, the public transport system, my course and what I had found in the wardrobe. Mundo wasn't really listening to me. I thought he was just pretending to pay attention but, a while later, as if he was thinking about something else, he asked me to show him my discovery. 'What discovery?' I asked. I suddenly realised what he was talking about. I got the envelopes and spread them out on the table. 'Those two ladies used to live here,' my uncle said. 'Now they live in the countryside near Navarro. Their daughter rents the flat to us.' Strange as it may seem, this was the first time I had connected those images with real flesh-and-blood people. Before that, the photos, the letters, the X-ray and the piano-learning guide had no people behind them. They were testimonies from another planet, traces of a distant civilisation.

★

I lasted just three months at the estate agency. 'You have no sense of urgency,' my now former boss said to me. He threw me out. I didn't really understand but I kept my mouth shut and put up with it, as Zulema had taught me. Then, I packed up my things and shut myself in the toilet to cry. On the upside I now had more free time, and I never get bored. I found things to do. One was to return to my discovery. I found out that the X-ray was of a knee. Mundo held it up against the light. He couldn't find any signs of fractures. One of the ladies must have had arthritis.

★

There were six letters. All written by different senders but all sent to the same recipient: Edda. The handwriting was alike. Not in their style but in other ways, different ways. How each writer experienced time, for example. This conditioned the lettering. They wrote about simple things, made promises, gave their opinions, recalled things, all backed up by the soundness of a syllogism. If I sniffed the letter, I could smell the hand that had written it. It was the perfume of another era. Similar to the fragrance Zulema used to wear in summer. All the letters had that atmosphere, what they described was the reflection of a different reality. In one, they spoke of a tree as if it were a man; in another, of a sudden south-easterly wind in El Tigre; in another, of holidays in the province of Córdoba; in another, they explained how to make rice pudding. There I was with my letters. Sprawled on the bed in Carlos Calvo. I read. I speculated. I immersed myself in Edda's story, which was sweeping and fragmentary, and hence, better than my own life. I crept gradually closer, like when I was little and wanted to catch a cricket, my heartbeat pounding in my ears.

*

One hot afternoon, the caretaker of the building invited me over to her place for an iced mate. She was plump, with bulging eyes, more oval than large. We both enjoyed watching one particular afternoon soap. We also liked avoiding our neighbours. These things created a bond between us. She smiled; I smiled. She was a chatterbox; I, a woman of few words. Gradually, almost reluctantly, I began talking. I asked her about the ladies who had lived in my flat. She remembered them but had trouble articulating herself. She didn't give me any useful information. I asked about Edda. The caretaker rolled her eyes. She sniffed the air just like a deer or a guanaco. She sucked the straw down to the last drop. Then, she moved closer as if she were about to kiss me. She said: 'Edda was wild. Bold. No one would dare step on her toes. Like Tita Merello.' She didn't have to say anything else. You could see the certainty in her eyes. From then on, in my eyes Edda would be Tita Merello, a woman who could settle on any shore. Or shape the shore to her liking.

★

I like to think there are hidden connections in life. Any act, for reasons unknown, can be connected to another act. One day I woke with toothache. I rushed to the dentist. I sat in the chair and opened my mouth. A guy with a poker face picked up some forceps at random. It was his métier. He felt powerful. He put in a temporary remedy. It fell out after a day and a half. He tried again. It lasted a week. Admitting defeat, he said: 'I recommend extraction.' He took the tooth out on a Saturday morning. Hearing the crunching of the bones and bursting into tears was one and the same act. Overflowing with emotion, the poker face said: 'It'll be over soon. Don't move.' I went home with half my face numbed by the anaesthetic. Every little while I probed my numb cheek with the tip of my tongue. I flopped down in front of the telly with Angela. She looked after me in her own way, with all the paraphernalia kids have around them. She brought me dolls, pencils and a paint box. She brought me water I didn't drink, an uncomfortable pillow, and a comb so she could comb my hair. I wouldn't let her. That was the first time I had ever been strict, and it went well, I was a natural. I hit the mark. Angela began to draw a dog but she wasn't pleased with how it turned out. In a fit of rage she ripped the paper into tiny pieces. Inconsolable, she shut herself away in her room. Thankful for a bit of space I went to lie down on my bed, which I had been dying to do ever since I got home.

★

Poor health modifies your perspective. I'm sure of it. Even something as routine as the discomfort after a tooth extraction. It changes the way you see things. It's like putting on new glasses. Everyone knows that the best place to read is in bed. In my case, I read magazines, whichever ones I can get my hands on, or that people lend me. I also read the letters sent to Edda. After the tooth extraction, I kept myself entertained with three in particular, which, in my opinion, were the best. One from a guy who tells her about making plum compote. Another from a relative who initially talked about property deeds but then lost their train of thought and ended up discussing a dog. The last one was the best of all, because you could only make out the gist of it. It was hard to grasp the meaning. It was written by a woman. She had kneaded the story as if it were a ball of clay. Then she flattened it out and it seemed like it had never existed.

The signature was also almost illegible. It seemed to say Ileana, but I'm not sure. The confusion was in the handwriting and the way she told a story. Everything was tangled up. A real fankle, as Zulema used to like to say. The letter was dated April 2010. It spoke of events that had happened more than a decade earlier. Ileana and Edda had shared a bedroom in a mansion, out in the country. That I understood: a curtain pinned to the wall, a ceiling fan, the smell of lavender mixed with carbolic soap, the song of the lapwings. And the somnolence of the siesta. It read: 'in sweet intimacy, the pleasant lethargy of the siesta'. Then, as if regretting what she had written, she changed the subject. She told stories about horses, and selling horses. But to finish the letter, as if her thoughts had taken on a life of their own, she returned to the subject of the bedroom. This time from a different angle: regret. She complained about the passing of time, that she had aged faster than she should have done. I tried to imagine Ileana's face. I'm not very creative and the face that came to mind was Zulema's. I thought about her crazy in love one summer afternoon. The other was Edda, whose image matched the photos, the picture of the patio. Both of them understand the importance of that siesta. They are somewhere remote. The ceiling fan barely ruffles the sheets. From outside comes the sound, not of silence, but of the stillness of the earth. Their eyes meet. Their gentle breathing has fallen into rhythm. They lie down, each in their own bed. They are forgotten to themselves. They talk of their little worlds as if they were vast. They smile. They smile at each other. They let time pass, they have no intention of sleeping. They would stay like this, just as they are, forever. One of them stands up. Or both, it doesn't matter. And in that precise moment, when it is neither hot nor cold, when nothing else exists, they understand that passion, against all volition, has chosen just the two of them.

TRAVEL, TRAVEL

1

After seven hours sitting on a bus he is now standing, straight as a rod, facing the front garden. He knows the house was built in 1922. He'd remembered that date as a child and has never forgotten it. He looks down. The journey weighs on him, a tingling in his joints. He turns his head to one side, then to the other, hoping – in vain – to relieve the tension in his neck.

He gazes at the flowerbed by the front door and imagines it barren. The soil has hardened. No one has taken care of it nor tilled the soil to allow it to breathe, awakening its potential for plants, insects, any seed hoping to germinate. There are overgrown weeds and the occasional wildflower. He's never really been interested in gardening; yet he's standing by the flowerbed, completely absorbed. He doesn't blink, or move. He feels removed from any overvalued intellectual thought. A suitcase hangs from one hand, an Adidas bag is slung over his shoulder.

It's half past three in the afternoon. A cool Wednesday. Above the roofs, above the checkerboard paving stones of the plaza, above the street – which is more of a track that narrows to a thread winding through the scrubland – hangs a forgettable sun, like a bauble.

He turns the key twice in the lock and enters the house. At once a strong musty smell hits him. He remembers the way to the kitchen, and there he does what is needed for the miracle to occur: he flicks the switch and the bulbs light up. Then, just as he used to do in this very place, he goes into the dining room dragging his feet. He's mastered the art of travelling without moving, as if he were on a gliding train. Since everything tires him, he pulls off one of the sheets covering the sofa with a single tug and flops down. He wants to rest for a minute, gather his strength, but ends up falling asleep. He sinks into a deep sleep with his head tilted to one side. Like all men, he snores. His brain is divided into two hemispheres; his heart encased in a thick patina, occasionally distracted by arrhythmia. His mouth is slightly open. The fingers of his right hand gently graze the floor.

2

The silence wakes him. His eyes roll in their sockets and he remembers where he is. The room is a country within another country. He straightens himself up, leans on his elbows, and becomes an exact image of the bureau, the table, the six chairs and all the things that have let themselves go in this place. He has a first name but everyone calls him by his surname; even his wife and his children, he has two. Canedo, they call him. He's someone who's sure of himself and his opinions. He looks people straight in the eye and talks straight. He has strived to create a belief system based on sincerity and the idea that certain things are unquestionable. When he speaks about these the strength of his faith can be observed even in the tiniest gesture he makes. Canedo is resolute in his self-belief. He also believes, as he has since he was a child, that speed is the greatest virtue. There's an episode in his past that explains this. When he was six, his father lost his job. He asked him why and his father responded: 'In this life you have to be quick off the mark.' As a kid, Canedo linked speed with skill. Today, faithful to this view, he loves technology: there's nothing faster than communications technology. He buys the latest tablets and smartphones. He's not interested in owning a status symbol, but in affirming himself in the present. The first productive thing he does that day is phone the internet company to arrange the Wi-Fi installation. He'll be online tomorrow.

He sits listening to the lapwings. Light seeps through the cracks in the door. It's the lethargic hour. He decides to get on with things, get a head start. He jumps up. He has things to do: phone his wife, let her know he got there okay, ask her how the kids are. He must air the house; examine this place that was his more than thirty years ago. Thanks to these chores, the next few hours will go by quickly. He'll then go and eat something at the service station bar he spotted from the bus. That's all he'll have time for today.

3

It's morning. He goes out through the backyard – a wild rectangle of weeds and two trees – and walks down a concrete path. A phone is stuck to his ear. He's talking to his wife. He doesn't pay attention to his surroundings. He could be walking through a desert for all he knows. He tells her that he found the house in a dilapidated state and is going to make some repairs. He wants to sell it as soon as possible and to the highest bidder. He says: 'I want to resolve this quickly and effectively.' She responds in monosyllables as she types on the computer. Canedo hears the tapping of the keyboard. That sound makes him wary: the things he's saying create a strange tension. He speaks about the damp climbing up one of the walls and mentions, at the same time, something he doesn't quite understand. It's a side effect, an undesired result. Under his tongue he conceals the pearl of a recurring argument. 'The kids are at school. Yesterday they brought home a stray cat,' she says. 'Yesterday?' he asks. 'They're crazy: a stray cat,' she says. 'They're just kids,' he says. 'It's dangerous,' she says. 'They're your children. Give them some boundaries. They're crying out for some,' he finishes. The stem of a plant peeks out of a can of grease. Canedo plays with it. He nudges it with his foot as if testing its resilience; he picks a leaf and brings it to his nose. He inhales. The phone is still stuck to his ear. The smell: camomile, field horsetail, mint. It reminds him of his mother when she used to cure him of the evil eye. She'd use a small pot with water and oil, her eyes would fill with tears, one yawn after another, as she'd babble an incomprehensible prayer.

He feels an urge to interrupt his wife. He'd like to tell her about this sudden memory. His desires mirror his insecurities. Now, she's talking. She's telling him something about damp towels; then she lists the problems with the freezer. Canedo says goodbye quickly and hangs up. He goes to the kitchen to prepare mate. He pours water two or three times and observes what the sky holds in store. First a change in light, a subtraction. Then, an uncomfortable breeze, like the prelude to a fight. 'Rain,' he says. 'Shit, a lost day.' He takes a look at the house, which is a disaster, and he has no idea where to start. He shakes his head. He brews another mate. He can see a bunch of clouds advancing from the west. He swipes the screen of his tablet and waits for the applications to load. Up to that point, he'd been enjoying his own company.

4

It is neither hot nor cold. The climate is dry. For Canedo this was no ordinary day of work. He employed strength and skill the whole day. He had trouble getting going, but once he overcame his initial resistance, his memories motivated him. He stripped one of the walls. He replaced two planks of wood on the veranda. His success emboldened him: he tinkered with the precarious electric wiring. He stopped for an hour and a half at midday. He ate some bread and ham for lunch while he Skyped with his wife. Then, he went out for a walk around the town. It horrified him that everything was just as he remembered it, and that this enduring character of things suggested not persistence, but rather apathy.

He walked for three blocks under the sun. A flock of sparrows flew from branch to branch. He walked calmly, at a slow pace. He was wearing old trainers and a sweatshirt spattered with paint. Before he reached Avenida San Martín he stopped at a corner shop. The guy behind the counter, the thinnest man in the world, recognised him at once. 'Is that you, Canito?' he asked. They hugged. He hurriedly improvised a summary of his life story, barely distorting the facts. He bought crackers, fruit, cheese, a 1.5-litre bottle of Coke.

It is seven in the evening and the bottle is almost empty. He's watching a comedy show on the old television set. He's really enjoying it. He roars with laughter and talks at the telly, letting out a stream of insults praising the actor's satirical talent. In one scene, he can't handle it any more: he grabs his stomach and doubles over in laughter. He's laughing so hard he starts crying. For no apparent reason he is overcome by a sense of wellbeing; a joy that moves through his body like a murmur until, at some point, it is transformed into exhaustion. 'I'm exhausted,' he says. He's drained. He grabs hold of a glass and can feel the blood flowing in his hand. Manual labour makes him real. Today he is more like his true self than ever before. Without a doubt, he inhabits the house that was his childhood. On the oilcloth-covered table are two apples. Beneath the kitchen sink, a puddle of water − which can be glimpsed through some flowery curtains − grows larger and larger.

For a week he's been trying to scrub up the house. Every day he feels better, stronger. He observes himself in the mirror and tries to note, even down to the tiniest detail, how the physical activity is changing his body. Yesterday he started work on the pitch pine in the dining room. He removed three strips. He spent a moment tracing the grain of the wood with the tips of his fingers. He wanted to understand its logic in order to succumb to the natural order. He is obliging with the world. He tries to behave as is proper. He undertakes casual mandates as if they were edicts.

He walks three blocks to the carpenter's. He struggles to make himself understood, which is more down to the noise of the power saw than the poor hearing of the guy at the counter. He perseveres. He finds what he's looking for. He waits for an hour for his order to be ready, and spends the time stroking a dog lying on its back by his feet. The sun is an enormous patch of light on the floor tiles. He accepts every sweet mate they offer him, savouring the taste as he listens to the radio, a contest of voices and static. He chats to the guy in the shop about football. Then about women and the wide diversity of sexual appetites. The conversation quickly becomes pure innuendo, an exchange of exaggerated ideas, codes that bring them together, an old and effective language.

He returns home with the wood over his shoulder. He struggles to accept that the working day is already drawing to a close. He tries to do a few things. He drags a bucket, prepares a cement mixture, uses a tape measure and plumb line, but is distracted by the smallest thing – the neighing of a horse, the song of a lapwing – and finds himself in front of his tablet. He chats to his wife. He tells her about his day, omitting the visit to the carpenter's. He finds out that one of his kids, the youngest, had a minor accident at school. It was during break time, a fall, nothing serious. He asks to talk to his son to hear his side of the story.

It is 23°C. There is a pleasant breeze. Not a cloud in the sky. Canedo is thankful he doesn't suffer the weight of gravity. Today the weather is merciful. He sits at a table in the centre of the room. He surveys his territory. Everything dismantled. There's a can of paint, piles of wood shavings, newspaper pages scattered over the floor, tools, boxes of nails. It's a work of art. He breathes in through his nose. He rubs his hands together, they feel gnarled, full of tendons, fibres, and blood. Canedo has transitioned from a temporary to a full life. He crossed the threshold almost without noticing. More than willpower or imagination, he has a different perception of time. He achieved this, without trying, through manual labour. His fingers took on a life of their own when he was connecting the wires of an electrical outlet.

He goes out into the street. He wants to distract himself with the hustle and bustle of the closing hours of the day. He knows that the shop sells stuffed flank steak and crusty bread. He knows that he'll turn 37 in two days. He intends to spend his birthday alone. He has a feeling his wife will raise a glass to him in his absence. She'll buy white wine, a Riesling, for the occasion. This simultaneity heartens him. He understands reality as an accumulation of layers, literally superimposed one on top of the other.

Time passes smoothly. It's been two weeks since he arrived. He's now 37. From the moment he turned 37 he felt like he had assumed, from one instant to the next, a new identity. He knows that this is related to his mood. This is a perception that is not backed up by any evidence, yet he supposes that such trivialities must be based on something genuine, a kind of truth that filters through the cracks. He also presumes that this is true across all ranks of life. This idea comes to him at two points of the day: in the morning, as he waits for the water to heat on the stove to prepare the four mates he drinks for breakfast, and, at the end of the day, when he puts his head under the stream of water that spurts from the tap in the backyard.

Today is Thursday. It's 10.43 a.m. It's a hot morning. He seeks refuge in patches of shade as he walks down the street. He's wearing a shirt and a pair of cargo trousers. He's been recommended a well-priced timber yard. He wants to check it out. On the way there, he comes across a pack of three dogs that appear to be in a hurry and an old man on a bike who greets him warmly. He nods his head in response, an acknowledgment barely perceptible. There's something suspicious about the old man's friendliness. He senses he's being made fun of. He distracts himself observing the magnificent sky and the crowns of the trees. But the truth is that since he arrived, he hasn't had a proper conversation with anybody. He's had exchanges of a practical nature but he hasn't spoken to anyone about anything specific or even just about any old nonsense. He misses having a good chat. The conversations he has with his wife over Skype don't cut it. Perhaps because this desire predisposes him, between today (Thursday) and tomorrow he is going to establish new connections with two people older than him, with whom he'll communicate on a deeper level. One of them will be key to his fate.

7

At 6.30 p.m. he undresses. He hesitates for a second before entering the wintry climate of the shower. The water emerges in a fine spray. Canedo's muscles contract. He's frozen stiff; he can't bear it. His body shakes violently. Since he arrived in town he's had problems with the boiler. He wants to install a 160-litre immersion heater. Discomfort is paradoxical. The cold, for example, takes his breath away, and at the same time revitalises him. He rubs his arms vigorously. For a second, he feels invincible, a man of steel: bad things can happen but they are of no real consequence. Soon he's out strolling in the evening air. He's combed his hair back with gel and is wearing a shirt that smells of lavender. It's light, loose, and makes him look like a character from a Scott Fitzgerald novel. He's in the front garden. He trims his nails with some clippers, then goes back into the house and is amazed by the versatility of a plastic tube.

His mobile phone rings. Irritated by the bad signal, he says 'hello'. It's his wife. For the umpteenth time he perceives how poor their conversation is. After going off on a few tangents, she says she wants to change one of the sofa covers. Canedo agrees. He says so and takes advantage of her brief pause to confess that he wants to come home, that he's tired of the town. 'Finish the repairs and put the house on the market. Then, you can come home with everything sorted,' she suggests. 'With everything sorted,' he repeats. They say goodbye affectionately.

He leaves his phone on a chair. A sudden lucidity sharpens his perceptions. The world is moving at a different speed; objects and beings are engaged in an activity all of their own, without aim or purpose. All at once he has a complete experience of movement. This is not something metaphysical, it is concrete, tangible. He assumes his wife's tone of voice refined his judgement. Then, he links his assumption with a chain of ideas. Although it may seem dumb – and that's how he sees it – this brand new structure calms him. 'What's happening to me is normal,' he says to himself. 'It's okay.'

He goes over to the window and looks outside. Nothing's changed: a welcoming lane, concrete, an Ika pickup truck, a sign that says 'bakery'. But he sees something else: a woman washing her hair in a tin basin. She's halfway down an alleyway between two houses. Canedo follows her movements. He watches her as she rinses her hair and then braids it into two plaits that get looped in a bun above the nape of her neck. He knows this woman. He knows her name is Helga, that her parents were born in Hungary, that when she was younger everyone called her the little Russian girl, that she must be around 65 years old. Canedo steps out to say hello. He asks her if she remembers him. Helga squints as she looks at his face which she doesn't take long to recognise. Not only does she remember him, but also his entire family. They make small talk. They avoid talking about the present and divert into the past. This is the first sign of mutual understanding. That evening, before 10 p.m., Helga crosses the road to his house. She has a good excuse. She brings a crème caramel covered with a tea towel. Canedo smiles and concedes. He accepts that destiny is a strange thing.

Helga and Canedo act like two boxers. They size each other up for nearly an hour. They end up in an old bed with a metal headboard. It is surrounded by bags of debris and piles of floor tiles. As Canedo thrusts to and fro on top of Helga his mind is completely blank. He kisses her neck as if his life depended on it. He's a castaway on a desert island. He searches for her mouth. After a while everything is calm. He rambles on about the pros of a new tablet. He concentrates on details he has trouble explaining. He doesn't really understand himself, but he keeps on talking. He's excited. Helga listens attentively. She dishes up the dessert and they eat in bed, from the only two plates in the house. Helga is wearing a flowery dressing gown. Her underwear is tangled up in the sheets.

8

The relationship lasts three dates. Each follows more or less the same pattern and, in fact, it is the routine that sustains their connection. To use an image: they pedal on a stationary bicycle. They move neither forwards nor backwards, but this stillness brings them comfort. Sometimes Canedo's mobile rings and he answers, getting lost in endless conversations with friends or relatives. In this dead time Helga bites her nails. She doesn't feel slighted. She's beyond good and evil. She herself likes to say, 'I'm beyond good and evil'. When he penetrates her, Helga squeals and insults him. 'You bastard,' she says. Then, they fall silent. He always falls asleep and snores until Helga builds up the courage and wakes him up. 'I'm leaving,' she says. 'I'm worn out,' he says, 'Exhausted.'

One Wednesday, Helga tells him that she's upset. She found her canary dead. She doesn't know what happened but thinks it was her cousin getting her own back. They recently had a fight over nothing. Canedo listens to her. He tucks a strand of hair behind her ear. Sweetly, he tries to cheer her up. Helga cries and covers her face with her hands, but a moment later she's alright again. Another day, Canedo buys himself some trousers. He asks her to take up the hem. She smiles, understandingly. She raises her face to the sky as if she had been waiting her entire life for someone to say those words. The night air is heavy. 'I think it's going to rain,' he says. After this, without rhyme or reason, the relationship falters. What's striking is that neither of them notices. She straightens the pillow and leaves. Canedo watches her walk towards the door in her worn-out body. It's the end. There are no reproaches. No drama. The next day, Helga hems the trousers. But she'll never be able to return them to Canedo.

9

It's Friday. He goes back to the timber yard. He found a cap at the back of a drawer. It's white and has a visor. He decided to use it to protect himself from the sun. At the yard, he bumps into the same old man who had greeted him a few days ago from his bike. The old man smiles and speaks to him. 'I knew you when you were a boy. I was a good friend of your father,' he says. Canedo listens to him as he's waiting to pay. He doesn't have much choice. The old guy talks about his father's favourite horse. 'A silver dapple that ran like hell,' he says. The story sounds familiar, he thinks he remembers hearing it over the dinner table during his childhood. The old man's way of speaking makes him feel comfortable. It immediately reverses the impression he had of him the other day. He thinks he could listen to him talk all day long.

From the yard they go to a café where they order coffee. The old man is a fountain of stories. He waves his hands in the air and talks loudly. He's smart and witty, focusing in on small details and, with impressive skill, transforming them into key features. He has a keen eye, Canedo thinks. The old man introduces him to everyone at the café. Affectionately. He treats him like a son. This way of relating to others builds a ramp along which Canedo races at top speed. He responds to the moment, without taking into account his own will or desires. His behaviour responds to their friendliness. The scene calls for music and Canedo dances along spontaneously.

In the street, they hug and slap each other on the back. They've just met but they're already close. Canedo walks a few steps towards the corner and hears the old man calling his name. He forgot to say something. He wants to invite him to a party organised by a friend in a country house four kilometres outside of town. It's that very evening. Can Canedo make it? The old man is sure he can. He makes things easy for him: he'll come and get him in his pickup at half past eight. Canedo declines, unconvincingly. The old man insists. 'I'll come by at eight thirty,' he says confidently.

On the way home, Canedo thinks about it. It won't do him any harm to have a bit of fun. He hardly does any work that day. He answers some emails, sorts out a couple of things. He moves the pieces of his life disinterestedly, a soul separated from its body. The delivery arrives from the timber yard early that evening. Two guys who barely say a word. Canedo gives them a tip and they take great pains over their work. They carefully arrange the materials they brought in the truck and sweep out part of the house. The work ends up looking as if it were further along than it really is.

He rubs his hands together. He's happy with the day's progress. He feels productive even though he's done very little. His good mood makes him sociable, communicative, so he calls his wife and they talk for longer than usual. She asks him if he's eating well. 'I'm cooking healthily,' he says. He makes sure to say the words she wants to hear. Then he tells her about meeting the old man. For the first time he realises he doesn't know his name. 'The old man,' he says. He's about to tell her he's going to go to a party with him that night, but he holds his tongue. It's something he's been doing more and more frequently.

10

The old man is punctual. His hands rest on the steering wheel. A second ago he honked twice to let Canedo know he'd arrived. Canedo leans out the window and calls that he'll be there in a moment, but he doesn't take any time at all.

Now they're in the pickup, driving through town. They're both wearing checked shirts and have combed their hair back with gel. The smell of cologne permeates the cab. They're versions, different shades, of the same model. They speak the bare minimum. They listen to music on the radio and the squeaking of the suspension. Initially the surface is tarmac, then gravel, then dirt.

Before they reach their destination Canedo discovers two things. The first is that the old enemy of his father is going to be there. The old man says 'Zenarruza' and the past comes tumbling back. A scene from his childhood. Screams and brutality. Two rabid dogs: Zenarruza and his father locked together in a cloud of dust. A fight to the death. Zenarruza is now 86 years old. The second is that someone is interested in the house. They want to meet him; preferably sort things out without an estate agent. They're not interested in the house but the land. This disheartens Canedo. He feels it is a threat to his memories; but he says nothing. He smiles and says: 'We'll kill two birds with one stone.'

They reach the country house, the party. The old guy flits from group to group. His hearty laugh rebounds from all sides. He gets a glass of wine for himself and another one for Canedo. Then he disappears into the crowd. The smoke from the barbecue and the music pumping from the speakers form a wave that engulfs everyone. Indifferent to the commotion, eleven horses graze at the back of the field.

There's a stage with three chairs and a microphone. Canedo leans against a post, taking sips of wine. He pretends to look busy so as to attract attention. He's successful: a brunette, about thirty, sets her eyes on him.

'It's you,' her eyes say. 'It's me,' his respond. They're in the middle of this when Canedo is approached by a couple. It's the people the old man spoke to him about. Their surname is Basque: Irungaray. They're just as he had imagined; although perhaps the guy is slightly ruddier, and perhaps the woman is slightly less weather-beaten. They get straight to the point and talk about the house. Canedo likes their forwardness, he associates it with spontaneity. Even though they don't reach a deal they establish the basis of an understanding. They have good chemistry. They drink wine and Fernet Branca mixed with Coke. They eat meat and different kinds of ham.

A man with an accordion gets onto the stage. He plays chamamé, swaying and letting out whoops of joy. The woman dances with her husband and then with Canedo. He tries to copy the steps of the dancers around him but he soon feels foolish. The night flows and their familiarity grows. They end up at a table by themselves talking about child-rearing. She argues that the basis of a good upbringing is strict parenting. 'Boundaries,' she emphasises. Canedo agrees and complains about how rude his children are. 'They're only young,' Irungaray comments, and stifles a yawn. It's almost three in the morning. So late. They all feel sluggish after eating. Time to go.

By this time of the night, the old man is nowhere to be seen. Canedo thought this might happen, but is now thrown by his absence. Around him, the party has reached its crescendo. 'Stupid old man,' he mutters. The Irungarays are talking amongst themselves. They seem to get on well. She strokes her husband's cheek with the back of her hand. The husband, in turn, dim-witted with alcohol, absorbs reality with apathy. He shifts in his seat and says: 'Let's go.' They'll give Canedo a lift back into town.

The Ford is covered in a thin layer of dust. Irungaray drives; his wife sits in the passenger seat. Canedo gets in the back, as best as he can, amongst a bunch of carrier bags. No one helps him, no one makes his life easier. He leans forward between the two front seats to participate in the conversation and observe the passing landscape. They drive through the countryside. It is pitch black. The car's headlights are fixed on the gravel road ahead.

A mile goes by. Now they're back on the paved road and the conversation falters. An uncomfortable silence falls. The wife attempts to restart the conversation, without success. She can't create the right atmosphere. She remains silent with her eyes fixed on the road. Irungaray has the window down. A cool mint breeze enters the car. The wife complains she is cold. 'Can you close the window?' she asks. Her husband doesn't hear or simply ignores her. A while later she asks again. Irungaray looks at her out of the corner of his eye. He says something that is simply and clearly a provocation. Or that's how Canedo interprets it. The woman reacts. 'You can't treat me like that,' she complains. The argument quickly escalates. Canedo has never felt so uncomfortable in his life. He shifts in his seat, amongst the carrier bags. He breathes in. He scratches his neck. 'Okay, okay. Let's all calm down,' he says. Then he does something foolish: he opens the window closest to him. The wind rushes into the car. For a second no one realises what is happening. That uncertainty, with its suddenness and its absurdity, enrages the adversaries. Harsh words are exchanged. They'll come to blows soon.

All Irungaray's attention is focused on the argument. He is no longer paying attention to the road. And so it happens. They take a sharp corner, the front tyre clips the verge, and the car loses control, spins around, then swerves across the road and crashes into a tree.

12

The sound of the crickets is the only thing he hears. Also a sleepless bird. Nothing else. The night is blacker than ever. The engine emits smoke and a strong smell of burnt oil. Canedo gets out of the car and walks toward a ceibo tree. He leans with one hand on the trunk and takes a moment to recover. Right away he checks his iPhone. No signal. He turns his phone off and on again with the same result. He says to himself: 'I've just been in an accident, my shoulder hurts, I don't have any signal, the people I was travelling with are dead.' But he's wrong: the couple only have cuts and grazes. Irungaray has a cut on his forehead; his wife scratches on her legs. They are frozen in shock. They are waxwork figures, flies trapped in amber. Suddenly, as if someone had given an order, they jump into action. She gets out of the car. She says: 'I can't believe it,' and then says it again, 'I can't believe it.' She cries and moans. Her husband runs to her side to console her. 'We're all fine,' he says, 'Calm down. Everything's alright.' The three of them look at each other. They go out of their way to re-establish a sense of normality. The accident was a temporal discontinuity, a fracture in the progression of time. The count has started over from zero.

She sits down. She says: 'My leg hurts. I need help.' They try and deal with the shock as best as they can. They don't take decisions, but wait for someone else to tell them what to do, where to go, what the right thing to do is in this situation. Then, Canedo reacts. He looks at the couple. 'I can't rely on them to sort this out,' he says to himself. He senses that there are people close by. He decides to go and look for help. He asks for more details about the area. He knows that there's marshland nearby and he's fearful that the night holds another misfortune. 'What direction is it in?' he asks. Irungaray gestures vaguely. Despite his disorientation, he leaves with a sense of hope. 'I'll be back soon with help', he assures them. They watch him disappear down a very dark path.

He is walking through a labyrinth. He wanders over difficult terrain. Canedo doesn't have the skill to navigate this territory. He observes the woods that consume him (the same tree a thousand times) and fails to draw a mental map. The humidity, the incessant humidity. He thinks he glimpses a clearing and takes off. He runs as fast as he can. He advances in a straight line for a few metres until he trips over something, and flailing his arms to try and keep his balance, he falls flat on his face. He tastes mud and blood. 'What the fuck did I hit?' he asks himself. He stands up, touches his lip and continues. The terrain is swampy. With each step his shoes make a sucking noise. 'Why on earth did I…?' he says out loud. He stops and checks his phone: no signal.

He feels like he has spent his entire life on this damned journey. Beyond some eucalyptus trees, he can see a path that snakes between shrubs that look like crouching men. Without giving it a second thought he takes the path. He says: 'I'm safe. Thank God.' He is parched. He strokes his throat to calm himself. 'It's nearly over. I'm almost there,' he says. He walks ten metres, at which point the path divides. He chooses the flatter path. To his right, the landscape is now clear. Canedo glimpses it out of the corner of his eye, but his gaze is focused ahead. 'It's the swamp,' he murmurs. He suddenly spots something moving ahead. He comes to a halt, terrified. It's a horse with its legs sunk up to its knees in the immense marshland. They make eye contact. The horse's eyes flash like a cat's. Canedo swears in surprise; although immediately he feels a twinge of responsibility. Then, he forgets the horse and continues on his way.

He walks briskly until the ground becomes uneven, but he maintains his course: he senses he's on the right path. Automatically, he adjusts his shirt and looks down at his shoes. When he looks up he notices the first light of sunrise. It is a light that seems unreal, but Canedo fails to take in this detail. He wants to reach a place where he can ask for help. So he carries on and doesn't stop to think about things he considers, at this stage in the game, mere distractions. It is only when he spots a human figure in the distance that he is startled. He doesn't stop to check. He raises his arms, shouts, does all he can to draw attention. The figure reciprocates, raising its arms, shouting and jumping. Canedo is grateful the person is willing to help, but the movements are so similar to his own he hesitates for a second. It seems to be a reflection or a mirage, as if an enormous mirror were refracting the landscape. So Canedo doubts. He stands still, motionless. He doesn't want even his eyelids to tremble. He tries to predict what the figure will do. The entire night has been difficult, but now, in this precise moment, the atmosphere has become unbearably tense.

JESSICA GALVER

Goldman is the director of the clinic. He makes decisions and not a hair on his head is disturbed. Sometimes his hypotheses are completely improbable, but then, no one can be right all of the time. Goldman comes to a conclusion and that's it. He didn't study a postgraduate degree in California for nothing. He knows the body's habits – the thickness of membranes, the length of the brainstem – yet he'll always take numerous factors into consideration. When he examines a patient, he doesn't restrict himself to the purely medical. Jessica Galver is a case in point: he included her in the trial because of an emotional factor. The patient has less fear of physical pain than of her own fear. For Jessica, the body itself is an illness, an incurable disease.

I can picture her. It's the first hour after noon. Eyes half-closed, her flabby, damaged hand shaking, she says that she would have liked to have been a rabbit. Her fat, equine body contorts beneath her mauve tunic; she sinks into a sudden stupor. That's her declaration of principles. In the evening, using the same words, I tell Simon about the incident. According to him, the key to Jessica's personality is the moment I just described.

★

41

One's position is extremely important. I'm valued. They ask me to stay. I'm standing beside the window and I get distracted. The garden stretches out, over the horizon, scarcely disturbed by islands of shrubs and, in the distance, a small grove of beech trees. The gardeners are at work. There are five of them. They don't speak, not amongst themselves, not to anyone. Each with their task, they all look like versions of the same man. I focus on one of them. His nose is enormous, faceted, various noses in one. He's bent over, his head glued to the ground. It looks like he's smelling the earth. His job is to keep the ants at bay. Every so often he raises his head and fixes his eyes on the horizon. Now, Goldman is observing me. He's behind his desk and it's essential that I focus my attention on what's happening inside the office. His eyebrows are bushy and unkempt, the only sign of carelessness in his appearance. His face is impeccably shaven; his hair, combed over to the right.

It's time. The director informs Jessica Galver that she'll be joining the clinical trial; she's the only patient in the whole clinic lucky enough to receive the treatment. We all congratulate her – Brodsky hugs her and pats her back – except Goldman, who coolly shakes her hand. He excuses himself with the same phrase he always uses.

The ceremony reaches its climax. No formality can avoid pathos. Jessica holds a pen in her hand, she leans over the contract papers and signs four times where she is told to. She doesn't bother with a close reading, skimming over the small print. She is euphoric. We all feel a little bit uncomfortable and shift in our places, taking small steps as if we can't decide whether to stay or go. Jessica grins from ear to ear. She couldn't be any happier. She is a beautiful, expansive woman. She weighs exactly 207 kilos.

First thing in the morning, I go into the room and open the curtains. Barely, just enough. A ray of light enters the room, hits the floor and tucks itself under the bed. Clothes lie on the chair: a dressing gown, a pair of tights, a light linen jacket. It is in these items that I see a body's habits. They are blissfully lethargic. Jessica is not a woman of the world or, as Simon would say, a woman in the world. She is covered by a sheet and her hair is spread loose over the pillow. She has the longest eyelashes I have ever seen in my life. She looks like a Hollywood actress from the 1950s. Naturally, she is a heavy sleeper. I nudge her arm to wake her. It's no use, I have to shake her.

As soon as she wakes up, she calls my name. She is less aware of me than I of her. She gathers her hair. She is a chrysalis, showing the first signs of transformation from its larva. Before she can say a word, I help her sit up. I grab her hands and pull her towards me until she is sitting upright. She adjusts the strap of her sleeveless nightgown. Her weight is an ethical philosophy, an aristocracy. She now makes use of it to stand up. She struggles, strains, ignores my outstretched hand. In the end she manages it. Her legs hold her up. She's standing tall and even her arms, which hang by her sides, gleam with victory. She breathes in and smiles with a hint of scorn.

She wants to chat, to be dramatic in the worst sense of the word. She resorts to what she has to hand. She tells me the story of one of her last dreams: a perverse Chinese artist is carving a piece of wood, he sinks his chisel into the wood and groans; she knows, even though no one told her, that she is his muse. I listen to her. The story has erotic overtones. I shrug my shoulders in confusion. In Jessica's childish, affected manner, in her surprise, in her choice of words, there is a certain hauteur. It's a kind of femininity, a deceitfulness I myself would like to possess.

★

I like routine. When I get home, I take a shower. I reproach myself for the smell of disinfectant I bring home with me from the clinic, as if I'd created it. With a lot of soap, the shower washes the smell away. Fifteen minutes later, I'm combing my hair in front of the mirror. Although I'm short-sighted, I note the effects of time on my face: my freckles have faded, my eyelids thinned. I make a list of trivial things which will disappear when I die. I list two or three in my head before I'm called back to earth. I get dressed – skirt and white blouse – and then steam some vegetables. Simon arrives home nearly half an hour later than usual. He's in a good mood. He gives me a quick kiss. I run my hand through his hair, my go-to sign of affection. We both realise how much we depend on one another: we're walking on a thin sheet of ice.

Simon is completely knackered. He's not really sporty, nor does he care that much about the environment, but he travels by bike. He's now in the bathroom. He comes out with sopping wet hair. I serve dinner while he looks around the house with his sad eyes. He's the voice of Walter White in *Breaking Bad* for Latin America. Today he did three episodes in a row. Dubbing is more than just his job, it's his calling.

He finishes his dinner and pushes his plate away. He fiddles with the ring he wears on the ring finger of his right hand. It's a tic he has when he's worried about something. I ask him what's wrong. He smiles as if he hasn't heard me and asks for some fruit. I watch him chew on an apple and I reflect on how little I know about his life: just a few facts. Simon is a complete mystery. And on this, which seems such an insignificant detail and is true for all men, I had founded my desire.

*

Brodsky can't roll his Rs. I don't understand him when he speaks. He gesticulates, points to the right and stammers something. He wants me to take Jessica Galver to consultation room 2. I know her schedule like the back of my hand. I know that today she has to have a load of tests but I delay the procedure anyway. Brodsky's face goes red. He hates me. Jessica is tired but in a good mood. Wrapped up in a blanket, I take her there in a wheelchair: the cold is a hallmark of the treatment.

Lying in the hospital bed, she looks paler than usual. Brodsky becomes all serious when he listens to her chest. A nurse takes the patient's arm, searches for a vein, inserts the needle and draws blood. Jessica Galver, extremely squeamish, turns away and looks out the window. She sees the morning in the crown of a tree. There are birds everywhere. I spot a robin on one of the branches. Jessica sees it too. She signals with her eyes to point it out to me. We've started to select the same things in the world. To me, she is luminous, flawless. She half-closes her eyes and gently takes my hand. Silently, she asks me to move closer. She whispers. She complains that she can't sleep. Brodsky brings our intimate moment to an end. He says her insomnia is a side effect of one of the drugs. He's an idiot. He thinks he knows everything, he's always got an answer on the tip of his tongue.

★

The rain is a curse. It's been pouring for two days. The water seeps through the air conditioning system into consultation room 1. It floods the room in minutes. The logic of the space is altered, the room becomes a different place while still remaining what it was. Measuring tubes, filters, trays, magnifying glasses float, forming a fleet that skirts the legs of the hospital beds and piles up against the wall. Strangely enough, the metal containers do not want to move from their places.

I'm standing in the entrance to the consultation room, watching the spectacle. Some ripples reach as far as my feet and then retreat. My soles are made of rubber: the shoes are part of my uniform. I'm with Goldman and a patient who is about to be discharged. A six-foot-tall German with a baritone voice. His name is Dirk. He works in vertical farming. During the time he's been in the clinic, all he's done is talk about his job. He seduced me, despite my best efforts, with his boring agronomist chat. As soon as he could, he threw himself on me. We used the bathroom. I leaned against the side of the basin and opened my legs. Dirk thrust blindly, like an ox. He's not fat like the other patients, but his spine is brittle and he has a tendency to put on weight. He slimmed down with our most basic treatment.

One of the housekeepers – I call her Dirty – came over and said something about the flooding. She looks at Dirk, then at me, then at Goldman. We don't respond. Out of nowhere, without the men seeing, she makes a face at me. She wants to tell me she has me in the palm of her hand, that she could ruin me whenever she feels like it. Goldman orders her to clean up the water, to wring out the cloths, to get on with it for the love of God. She smiles complacently.

A taxi pulls up in the driveway outside the reception. Goldman carries Dirk's suitcase and puts it in the boot. The German walks purposefully to the car, opens the door, but pauses for a second before getting in. He cranes his neck and looks. He shakes his head in disapproval at the terrible weather: there's something unjust about the way it is raining. Dirk was in the clinic for five weeks – we took great care of him – and now he's leaving and abandoning a world in danger, an order about to collapse. The water lashes against the building. At last, Dirk decides to get into the car. The taxi, one of those new Chevrolets, disappears round the bend.

*

It's six in the evening on Monday. I'm alone. Simon's not coming round today. I go out on the balcony. I have a bottle of water in my hand; the smell of medicine on my body. I look at an apple core. On a terrace, a woman is cutting her nails. There's something about her stillness that places her centre stage.

Sometimes my chest fills with a sense of wellbeing. In those moments I think I've planned my life well. I'm comfortable, within the limits of my freedom. The weather is mild and the sun is setting.

An hour ago, when I got home I saw a letter lying on the floor. I put it on the table to read later. I know it's from my father. No one writes letters these days. My father is a dinosaur. He lives in a town in the province of Entre Ríos, he moved there fifteen years ago. Every so often he phones me, but he prefers to write. He has neat handwriting, he separates every sentence as if they were chords. He comments on trivial things, daily occurrences. His stories always cast him in a good light. He tells me about the things he mends at home: the cable of the bedside lamp, a roof tile, a plug. And yet, strangely, in what he writes, two things become clear: a recurrent demand and an enduring mandate.

★

7.25 in the morning. The fourteen patients, Brodsky and I are on the bus. Adriana O. is complaining about the road; her complaint is unjustified: we're going at barely 30 kilometres an hour along a paved road. The driver, who is the spitting image of Matthew McConaughey, looks at us with hatred. We're undesirables. A disturbing group, a defect of nature, something that has to be fought against. He adjusts his Ray-Bans and shakes his head in annoyance. It's time I doubled down. I talk loudly. I laugh. I show my teeth. I'm acting crazy. Brodsky asks me to calm down.

We pull over in the shade of some poplars. We help the patients get out. They slowly drag themselves down the four steps of the bus until their feet touch the ground. Their obesity – not one of them is under 200 kilos – makes them weightless. Between one step and another they are suspended in mid-air. It's their idea of pleasure. I stay by Jessica Galver's side. We walk along a gravel path and she tells me stories about her mother. Birds accompany us. They're Jessica's chorus. I tell her and she laughs at the suggestion. 'No, no, no, sweetheart,' she says, as if she were my mother.

A few steps more and we pause to do some respiratory exercises. Brodsky stands in front of the group and leads. We raise our arms and the oxygen – as if it acted deliberately, of its own accord – fills our lungs. We feel a bit faint, just a little, a weakness in our shoulders. I observe Jessica. Her cheeks are flushed. Her skin is completely devoid of history. In a whisper, I ask her to look inside herself, to imagine her nervous system, her bronchial tree expanding, the tightness of her pericardium. She looks at me and smiles. She softly sings a few verses of *Madreselvas en flor*. Her voice is sweet, high-pitched.

We continue walking. It takes us twenty minutes to advance a handful of metres. I find out that Jessica has a ring that used to belong to her mother. She carries it in a locket: it's too small for her fingers. We reach the edge of a gully and pause for a second time. In the distance, a sudden wind flutters some bunting strung between two posts. We stand there, thoughtfully. Someone, not Brodsky, remarks that it's a mistake to move too quickly. 'At the end of the day, anything, cinema for example, is faster than life,' they say.

★

The letters my father writes are variations on the same theme. I understand him better now than before. Like him, I'm astute – not cunning, astute – in my dealings with the world. He tells me that he's made a wooden ramp to avoid having to use the stairs. He has a problem with his leg, pain along his sciatic nerve. He says: 'I made it in record time.' He says: 'A carpenter praised my work.' He repeats: 'A carpenter said it was well made.'

My father and I observe each other from a distance. We're parallel horizontal lines, like two boats on the same coordinate plane. We're aware of the dangers of the journey, yet we agree it would be in bad taste to mention them or have any survival strategies at the ready.

★

Simon has the memory of an elephant. He's standing beside the window in the living room. He's reciting a monologue from Chekhov's *Platonov*. Every once in a while, he stops to take a breath and a sip of lemonade. He brushes his hair out of his eyes. And continues. He's managed to land himself two more dubbing jobs on top of the Walter White gig: he has hardly any time for anything. He read Chekhov's play on the bus and memorised every word, even the commas. I listen to him attentively. Something he says reminds me that I'd cut Jessica's nails this morning. She entrusts me with her dainty hands like she would no one else. She likes to put them on display.

As I was gathering my things to leave, she asked me to remove her cuticles. It's something she enjoys. I pushed them back with an orange stick. She bites the corner of her lower lip. Pure pleasure. Jessica's as vain as she is fat. She never reveals her real age. She tends to take off a few years. I checked her medical history: she's 37. She has a child-like quality that keeps her young. It's no pretence, simply part of her nature, time is on her side. She told me that when she was eighteen she was happy for the first time. That's why she's remained in the flush of youth. As she said this, the sun flooded the room. We floated in its radiance.

★

Their calories are strictly counted. Jessica asks for her food to be taken to her room. She is a very particular woman, her interaction with the other patients is nil. There's a bunch of flowers on the table they've set up for her. Jessica is taller than I am. She is standing in front of the mirror. She rubs her eyelids with her fingertips. She seems anxious. A pink stain extends from her neck to behind her ear. She tells me something bit her while she was asleep. It's a rash. Her expression is a call for help. Like all sick people, she wants to be the centre of attention. She describes her skin problems as if they were large-scale historical changes, seminal events, History with a capital H. Her acne is like a revolution: outbreaks of pustules, swelling, abrupt changes in temperature; a violent reaction, out of proportion, an unforeseen epidemic.

I rub calamine lotion on her skin and the redness starts to go down. Jessica half-closes her eyes. She sighs. She's lying down comfortably, her head inclined leftwards, her chin as round as a peach. In the cleavage of her gown you can make out her white, autonomous breasts. They're so big they don't seem human. I stroke her right breast, run my fingers over it and play with her nipple. It's an immensely tender gesture, a woman-to-woman caress I've never given anyone else in my life. Jessica closes her eyes. She thanks me with a stifled giggle. A while later, Dirty enters the room – something unheard of – with the lunch tray. She looks at me as she always does, but this time I notice something different – a flash in her eyes – which tells me she is capable of anything.

★

Jessica always knew that the treatment was going to be painful. Today Brodsky rudely told her to stop complaining. 'You signed the consent form,' he reminded her. Jessica sighed, although that didn't mean she was giving in. She's now sitting on the edge of the pool they set up in the room with mirrors, beside the boiler room. The water is freezing. It was chilled with the ice I bought at the service station. Before Jessica plunges into hell, I give her a spoonful of glucose without anyone seeing. I then take two steps back and the nurses help her get into the pool. She screams when her foot touches the water, screams when they force her to sit down and screams when they wet her hair. From a distance I give her a comforting look. Brodsky checks her pulse and takes her blood pressure. He's more serious than usual. Jessica's skin is rapidly turning blue. The first session lasts for 46 seconds, but it's too much for her. She is almost fainting, her eyes glaze over. We pull her out, wrap her in towels and rub her hard. She says she can't take any more. She lets out a sob without shedding a tear.

Back in her room, we lie her down and cover her with a sheet. As soon as she feels a bit better she asks for more covers. 'Give me a blanket, sweetheart, I'm freezing,' she says to me. Brodsky shakes his head but I pretend not to notice: Jessica's pitiful face is heartbreaking. I grab a blanket and wrap it round her. Brodsky yanks it off the bed. In the corridor he corners me. He says that's the last time I disobey him, that I just don't get it, that I'm the bottom of the barrel. With me he reveals an old grudge he doesn't show to those who humiliate him.

★

Simon takes a bag of prawns out of the freezer. He knows his way around my kitchen as if it were his own. The light from the fluorescent tube is merciless, emphasising the bags under his eyes. While he makes the sauce he tells me about *Platonov*. His voice is too high-pitched for a man and becomes distorted when he gets excited. He sounds as if he were speaking through a tin can. I wonder how he could learn the entire play in just one reading. His memory is his talent. He repeats extracts from one of the monologues over and over again.

I met Simon in a self-help support group for people trying to quit smoking. I was impressed by his height and the thickness of his beard. He opens a bottle of white wine and pours two glasses. We have our ways of enjoying ourselves, but don't really understand each other. We clink our glasses and say cheers. Simon uses too much oil when he cooks. I repeat something I heard Goldman say in one of his talks. I make his words mine. I speak about the importance of a healthy diet. Simon cuts an onion and starts frying it. He smiles. And his smile weakens my argument: what I'm saying doesn't seem important.

We sit facing each other at the kitchen table. The prawns steam on our plates. *Platonov*: Anton Chekhov's first play. It's extremely long: written to be performed for eight hours non-stop. Simon is fascinated by excessive, strange things. He speaks about Chekhov as if he were his friend. I'm not really paying attention. I think about Goldman, his rules for running the clinic; then I think about Dirk, the agronomist, who follows the same rules of desire. Push, thrust, open with your fingers. Chekhov's first and last works were plays, Simon tells me. A car passes down the street: the kitchen transforms into a play of reflections. Dirk refused to look at the blister packs, he didn't want to know how many pills he was taking. I pay attention to trivial things. The most important things in life are the small details, and paying your rent, Brodsky likes to say.

★

They immersed Jessica in the freezing water a second time. She only lasted 67 seconds before her body began to decompensate. Her heart started beating like a runaway horse, reaching 190. They wouldn't let me in the room to help her because supposedly I'm no help during this stage of the treatment. I got annoyed. I told Goldman he couldn't separate me from my patient. He adjusted his tie and remained silent. Just then a heavy storm broke: recently it's been raining every other day.

Goldman asked me to join him for a cup of coffee at the roadside café. We carried one of those umbrellas that look like parasols. Goldman has good judgement: he values my work at the clinic. He talks non-stop about the SUV he's just bought. A stray strand of wet hair falls over his forehead. He asks me about my life, about Simon, my interests. He makes it clear that the clinic couldn't do without me, that it's extremely important I understand certain aspects of medical decision-making. Without me asking for it, he hands over a scientific paper that provides the medical evidence for Jessica's treatment plan. His action surprised me. I look up and watch a Scania truck pass by. Goldman, who doesn't take his eyes off the table, asks me to stay and read the paper carefully. He gets up, pays for the coffees and leaves. Exposure to extreme cold stimulates the metabolism. It produces oxidative stress in the particles of the adipose tissue. According to this study, Jessica's sacrifice makes sense. As I read, a constant stream of trucks pass along the road. The sound of the traffic is my background music, my mantra.

★

Thoughts pile up in no particular order. They stack on top of each other, overlapping, but maintaining their independence. They don't mix. I perceive this clearly as I gaze at my nails. They are painted. I painted my mouth a pale pink.

Yesterday Dirk phoned me. He made up an excuse and ended up asking me to meet him in a hotel in the centre of town. Initially I felt uncomfortable, really uncomfortable: the idea of meeting up seemed crazy, but then, I don't know why, I ended up giving in. I'm now sitting in the hotel bar. I'm drinking tea and pretending to be the kind of woman I'll never be.

Dirk enters the hotel lobby. Suddenly his huge frame blocks out the light of the day. He stands still for a few seconds until he spots me. He walks briskly. He's holding an old-fashioned diary with a leather strap and a packet of tissues. He's surprised to see me. What a cliché: he thinks women always arrive late. I compliment him on the jacket he's wearing: a blazer that perfectly matches his pristine white shirt. He thanks me and realises he has to return the compliment. He says something stupid about my hoop earrings. He then talks about work. He's impatient. He doesn't know how to control his desire. He wants me naked in the room his secretary booked. He struggles for a while with his role as seducer until all of a sudden I say: 'Shall we go up?' Dirk can't believe his luck. In the lift we kiss; in this desire there's a kind of instant happiness, as if there were nothing better in the world. I swallow, my breathing is agitated. Dirk doesn't know what to do with his hands. In his eyes impatience and lust converge. He must be asking himself how to take advantage of such good fortune.

★

He uses Chekhov's works as if they were the hexagrams of the *I Ching*. The universe is governed by a struggle between opposing forces. Seen through this lens, the majority of texts are prophetic and moral. He says to me: 'Look,' and opens the book at random. He reads a line of dialogue. The content always seems to miraculously speak about his current situation and predict an outcome. This makes things easy for Simon, it limits his future possibilities. He likes to think his actions respond to a logic that is not arbitrary. This is how he got the dubbing job. The voice of Walter White is not just any old voice. Simon is obsessed with his role. He stays in character even off stage. A blue vein twitches in his boyish neck. His eyelashes extend. My Simon, in those moments, seems like a doll that has come to life.

★

Jessica lifts her right foot three centimetres off the ground. She is barefoot. She steps onto the scales that Goldman bought in Rome. The room is tense. Brodsky's forehead is shiny with lack of sleep, he can't stop clearing his throat. His mouth has taken the form of the words he constantly repeats. His favourite is 'conspiracy'. His cheeks bulge as if he were sucking in air to whistle. There are five of us in the consultation room: Goldman, Brodsky, a nurse, a cardiologist and me.

Jessica smiles modestly; this modesty is balanced, classical, it assigns her to an ordained place in a harmonious world. She's standing on the metal base of the scales. Her linen jacket is draped around her shoulders, over her negligee. I notice this at the same time as Goldman. He asks me in a low voice to remove the garment. Nothing can alter the results.

The weights take their time to settle down and the anxiety in the room increases. Jessica, on the scales, is a monument. Her body – the size of this three-dimensional organism – is a spectacle. It's a representation, a *mise-en-scène*, the finale of an opera. But when we hear the number the frustration throws us off balance. Jessica has lost 300 grams. Just 300 grams. Goldman interprets this as a clear sign of injustice in the world. 'What did we do wrong?' he asks himself. But I know – we all know – that he is looking for culprits. To eliminate any doubt, Brodsky defends himself. He speaks about her exposure to the cold. It must be more regular, he reflects. The nurse and I take care of the patient. She seems less bothered by this failure than we are. She makes a comment about her health: what she says is neither true nor false. We wrap her up, not because she's cold but so we have something to do. The doctors can't take their eyes off the patient. They watch her little, fat head. 'If you don't help yourself, there's no treatment that can help you,' Goldman lectures her. The remark washes over Jessica. She shrugs her shoulders. According to the medical protocol, hostility helps the patient lose weight: they should be mistreated. Abuse, when it is methodical and focused, is a weapon against obesity. In the majority of cases, the ideas that rule the world are ludicrous.

★

Today was a hard day at the clinic. I go into the changing room and Dirty's in there. She's in her underwear in front of her locker. She's changing out of her uniform. I immediately notice that her bra straps are worn. She pretends she hasn't seen me. She raises her head like a deer and puts on a patterned T-shirt. I can smell her. She turns away and pretends that what she's doing – getting dressed – takes up all her attention. It's a sign of weakness. With this insignificant detail I organise my plan. I walk towards the centre of the room. I look confident. I say hello loudly, as if there were a lot of people present. Dirty looks at me, disconcerted. She doesn't realise that this is my way of ignoring her. I try to exploit her negative energy in my favour.

She jumps up as if she's been stung. She puts her uniform in her bag and just as she's about to leave something makes her change her mind. She can't be beaten that easily. She says something stupid and gives me a challenging look. Up close Dirty is a brute. Her face looks like it was carved in stone. 'I know things about you,' she says. I place my clothes in my locker. I try to forget she exists. 'Listen to me, slut,' she says. I stare at her with all the hatred I can muster, but it's not enough, not even all the hate in the world would stop her: she's up for a fight. 'I saw you with the German guy,' she says. 'The walls have eyes,' I think. I have no idea what to do, so I shake my head. I try to maintain my self-control but I can't help trembling. She prods my shoulder so I can't ignore her. She gives details: 'I saw how the German spread your legs; you were enjoying yourself like a whore.'

Dirty has a birth mark over her eyebrow. It turns purple when she gets angry. She takes advantage of my silence and comes closer. As she speaks – more details about my rendezvous with Dirk – her spittle hits me in the face. 'I can't handle any more of this,' I think. 'This idiot is not going to mess things up for me.' 'Pretend you can't hear her,' I tell myself. But I can't tolerate her insults. I inhale deeply and hold my breath. I wait for a few seconds to clear my mind. I close my eyes. When I've calmed down I open them again. But I'm not calm at all. In fact, I'm bursting with rage. I shout at the top of my lungs: 'All men want me, you fucking idiot.' But it's not me who's speaking. Something, an external force, takes control of my voice and says those words. It's an outburst, an animal impulse, an ancient force. Dirty takes three steps backwards. She bumps into the door, her back against the wood. She looks at me with her mouth open. Suddenly she understands who I really am.

★

Jessica has all the time in the world. She sees what other people overlook. She points at the dust that spins in a ray of sunlight. 'Look,' she says, without saying anything else. She's only just woken up. We help her get out of bed. The nurse and I. As the days go by her movements become more and more restricted. Since last week, I've had to help her go to the bathroom. When she urinates, she grips my hand and half-closes her eyes. Her sphincter relaxes and the liquid flows. She hums a romantic song.

She's now back in bed. The treatment plan prescribes fortnightly transfusions. The blood leaves through one line and enters through another. There are tasks that become meaningless as the years go by; the transfusion becomes counterproductive after a few minutes. It's an illogical activity. Endorsing this lie implicates us all; yet we don't say anything. We do what we're told without saying a word. Jessica breathes slowly. She complains of a pain in her arm. We have strict instructions: we must ignore her complaints. The cardiologist has his ear on the stethoscope and his eye on the monitor.

Behind me, Brodsky dreams of promotion. He's not realistic. This characteristic of his constructs and protects him, it makes him who he is. The tube lighting is relentless. It beats down on us, making us look unnatural. Especially Jessica, lying on her back and unable to move a muscle. 'Beautiful Jessica,' I want to say to her. Her body is fiercely abundant but not remotely grotesque. Her corpulence is an ornament, the perfect accessory.

In two hours she has to be injected with an imported drug. It hasn't arrived from the lab yet. They send a motorbike with each injection. They don't want to break the cold chain, they say. They take extra care, they're worried about getting sued.

★

Repetition is preservation. Five days a week, I get up at the same time. I shower, have breakfast and go to the clinic. More than a job, it's a need. At eleven in the morning I have a cup of tea in the office. At that moment, I conceptualise my life as one endless cycle, the same day over and over. There are only a few, acceptable variations. Trivialities. Exceptional nothings. A change in the façade of the building, for example. Or a trip. Or, recently, my dates with Dirk. That. Nothing else. False moves.

Simon, in contrast, has other habits. He validates

himself in front of the mirror. He repeats his lines, he gives his all to his character. When he acts part of his identity is at stake, yet he's not at risk, it's his get out of jail free card. Theatre as freedom. In everything else he's just like me. To give just one example, in bed he's really unadventurous. For Simon, an orgasm is an act of memory: the same position, the same setting. Everything must be in order for the discharge to take place.

Not long ago he recounted a dream. He was the only character. He was on a ship roaming through space. He had no idea how he had got there. Darkness and weightlessness were one and the same. Suddenly, he realised that this was death, his death. The capsule, the spaceship itself, signified a sentence: perfect solitude. He would suffer this torture for eternity. There was no way of escaping this isolation. He woke with a start. He tore his sheets off and jumped out of bed. He couldn't shake off the sense of desperation: the image was too real, it exceeded the boundaries of a dream. To him, this dream death was real. He had to fight. Sometimes things get out of hand. Even the most harmless detail becomes a threat.

★

Goldman gave me instructions about the new drug. I'd also done my own research. I know how to administer it and what to do when it's in the bloodstream. It has an oily consistency; it causes hematomas and makes the skin bruise. It has to be applied with a thick needle. Once the needle's inserted you have to put pressure on the area. In the medical literature there are reports of bronchial spasms. Also of cardiovascular problems associated with the pain: not only is the injection painful, the torment continues as the body metabolises the drug. The physical discomfort can include pain in the limbs, tightness in the chest, photophobia and, occasionally, dizziness. It can also cause emotional disorders. It is recommended that the drug is combined with tricyclic antidepressants.

Jessica starts to cry as soon as the needle is inserted. The pain makes her tremble. She says: 'I can't handle it any more.' She pulls a face like a child. She whimpers and it makes me want to give her a hug. I don't do it: the protocol stipulates maintaining distance from the patient. The emotional factor is an essential part of the treatment. When she feels a little better we go to the park. We walk. Movement helps the drug circulate through the bloodstream.

Jessica doesn't say much. She says she can't cope, that she's reaching breaking point. I neither agree nor disagree. As we walk down a path, she gazes into the distance and moans. 'My chest hurts,' she says. I ignore her. 'Is it normal for my chest to hurt?' she asks me. 'You need to speak to Dr Goldman about that,' I respond. I know my change in attitude upsets her but I have no other option. One of the gardeners stops to watch us go past, he's cutting branches with a saw. Jessica is wearing a sleeveless blouse. Her arms are festooned with purple blotches. The last time she was weighed, she'd only lost only one kilo. She takes five steps and stops. She has difficulty breathing. She's a Renaissance Madonna. She places her hand on her chest. Half-closes her eyes. She gulps mouthfuls of air. Her permanently pale lips barely close. Someone is listening to the radio. The electric voice of the radio announcer floats towards us.

★

Simon normally has at least one foot firmly on the ground, but recently he's had both feet in the air. Three weeks ago his best friend got him all excited about a motorbike. 'I can't afford it,' Simon had said. His friend insisted, 'I'll lend you the money.' A teenage impulsiveness hung over the purchase: he confused the intensity of passion with the vertigo of speed. Simon now owns a Ninja 600.

He comes to pick me up to go on an outing to the countryside, I don't know where. The destination is just an excuse, what's really important is the journey. 'Feel the power of the 16-valve engine between your legs,' Simon says. The bike came with two full-face helmets, mine is pink. It suffocates me, I can't stand it. The road is so windy it blocks out any sensation of speed. Every so often Simon speaks to me, giving me instructions about how to ride pillion. I'm not listening to him. That's why I remain silent, although it's also because I'm terrified.

When we get to our destination a man in a flat cap is there to greet us. He hugs us as if he'd known us for years. He is taller than us; and uses this in his favour. Simon is obviously his inferior. We take a few steps and I find out he's a theatre director. We walk towards a table full of actors. When we arrive I realise their hands are greasy from preparing offal. I try to socialise. I gulp down a slice of meat and take a sip of wine. Then I discreetly sneak away. I throw myself down in the shade of some trees to try and shake off the motorbike journey. The branches wave in the breeze. My eyes start to feel heavy watching the insects buzz around in the air. Simon lies down beside me. 'What are you doing?' he asks. I breathe deeply: slowly emptying myself out. I see a lemon tree, and some bare branches wrapped around a gate, which look like orange blossom. As soon as I have the energy I tell him about Jessica's treatment: the freezing immersion baths, the abuse, the intravenous drugs. I imitate the way the plants have of creating the world. Simon stares at me. 'That's torture. I don't know how she bears it,' he says. And he speaks, without realising – he loves his job – in the same voice he uses when he does the voice of Walter White.

★

I'm in Goldman's office. I'm someone he trusts. He tells me about a change in the treatment plan. The cardiologist has advised us to stop the immersion baths. Jessica's heart is small for the size of her body. In the last session they registered an irregular heart rhythm, something quite common, nothing pathological, but they – and by them I mean the institute – don't want to take any chances. 'No one has ever died here,' Goldman likes to boast. Today he's wearing a blue tie with yellow crests I've never seen before. Goldman's eyes, like all scientists' eyes, are designed to spot the fine detail. The causes of things, aetiology, sudden discoveries, concern him. He now gives me a mission. I have to observe Jessica's pupils regularly. They have been dilated for two days. Goldman doesn't know why. None of the drugs used in the treatment list this as a side effect. He also asks me to accompany her to the toilet. I have to check the colour of her urine. Jessica cannot be permitted her privacy. 'Her body is more ours than it is hers,' Goldman says.

The meeting ends. I go out into the gardens to get some fresh air. The afternoon air partly reenergises me. The sky is clear. Not a cloud in sight. It's a spring sky in autumn. There's a flock of birds. They fly from left to right. They come and go. Suddenly, they disappear. I'm so distracted by the birds I don't notice the gardeners until, unexpectedly, one starts up a grass trimmer. He's trimming the edges of one of the paths. Further behind him there's another gardener. At first glance I think he's alone, but on closer inspection I realise he's with a woman. It's Dirty. I say her name, 'Dirty,' and the word gets stuck in my throat. They're deep in conversation. I imagine they're lovers but quickly reject the idea. There's no sexual tension, something else unites them. I think, I'm almost 100% certain, they share a secret. Something few people know. When they spot me watching them, they pretend not to notice. I convince myself that they're talking about me. Dirty is telling others what she saw me doing with Dirk. She's rehearsing. Imagining what it'll be like to tell Goldman. She fails to picture it. The gardener watches me from a distance. Tomorrow, when I run into him, he'll try to find some sign of perversion in me. He's just a lowly gardener. But still, it worries me.

★

Jessica is looking worse. Her pupils are the size of dinner plates. I give her an injection first thing in the morning. She complains about the cold. We wander around the clinic. Outside an angry wind rages. 'At least it's not raining,' I say. She shrugs her shoulders as if she doesn't care.

'My body aches,' she moans. We bump into the patients leaving the dining room. They waddle towards us. It's a familiar dance. One of the men greets us with a lewd expression. 'What's that fatso's problem?' Jessica remarks. The blotches from the new drug now cover her neck. She wipes her mouth with a towel. She's fastidiously clean and tidy. 'I can't handle the treatment any more. I want to quit,' she says. I ignore what she says. She stops to take a breath. On her chin, she has a blotch the shape of Australia. One idea leads to another. 'Jessica is a vast continent,' I think. If it wasn't against the rules I'd give her a hug, smother her with kisses.

Someone speaks over the intercom. After a couple of seconds I recognise Brodsky's voice. We have to report to consultation room 6. We both react as if we were in trouble and make our way over there. When we get there Brodsky is on edge. 'Where were you?' he asks. The light in the room blinds us. It's a searchlight, a dazzling brightness. Brodsky points at the bed. Twelve elastic bandages are laid out neatly. We're continuing with the thermotherapy. 'These are bandages impregnated with three different types of alcohol,' he informs us. 'Ice bandages,' he clarifies. Jessica shakes her head. 'Enough. I can't take any more,' she pleads. Brodsky goes over to the desk, opens a drawer and takes out some papers. It's like a scene in a play. 'Here's your written permission,' he says to her, waving the documents in the air. 'Don't give in to negative feelings,' he suggests. Jessica turns her head. The skin on her neck smooths out, tightens. It's a flash, a spark. With that gesture she plants herself firmly in the present, she puts her foot down, becomes more self-assured.

★

The clinic is only about 40 minutes outside the city, but it feels like the depths of the countryside. I get off the train. A woman wearing a scarf on her head is selling home-made bread. Crusty white rolls. It's morning. I buy one. I eat it as I walk towards the clinic. When I get there, I give what's left to the doorman, who thanks me with a frown, as if accepting the bread is humiliating. I go inside, get changed – my uniform is neatly pressed – and I pour myself a cup of coffee: someone in this world is in their correct place and fulfilling their duty. I look over Jessica's schedule; I check she's in the breakfast room. I've got loads of time, so I relax.

I send Simon a message, three words. I've got nothing I particularly want to say to him; I just say hi. He doesn't answer. Somewhere in the clinic a builder is using an angle grinder. Damn noise follows me everywhere: here, at home, anywhere I go. Simon doesn't answer and a feeling of anxiety creeps from my gut to my chest; now I taste it in my mouth. A bitter lemon pastille. It's unusual but it'll pass. I try to think about something else. My relationship with men has nothing to do with experience, it is pure indulgence. With Dirk, for example, I don't care if he's there or not, but his desire sustains me. That's just how it is.

Muzak is so ridiculous I only notice it when it disappears. Abruptly, a voice takes its place. It asks me to report to the director's office. Its tone is formal, it doesn't 'ask', it 'requests my presence'. Adding: 'Urgent.' I listen to the message and my mouth opens in surprise. I'm shocked, as if I'd been hit on the head, and the office I'm in – so disinfected and sterile, and permeated by the words that came out of the speaker – brings back a scene from my adolescence.

I knock on the door three times, no response. I wait but no one lets me in. Another three knocks: complete silence. It gives the impression the office is empty. I wait for a second and then decide: I have to check if anyone's in there. I turn the handle. I peek my head around the door and I see Goldman without his jacket on, wearing glasses. He's reading a hardcover book. It's an endocrinology handbook. 'I was waiting for you,' he says. He organises his things and motions for me to take a seat.

Goldman's eyes are sunken. He moves his lips as if they hurt. I tremble. 'My time's up,' I think. I relate this idea to the hostility of my surroundings. 'Anything is possible,' I think. Goldman has trouble speaking. He takes a deep breath and makes up his mind. In just a few words he tells me that Dirty has been fired. 'The woman from housekeeping,' he clarifies, just in case. I bite one of my nails. I suspect this is a game to try and get a reaction out of me. I'm mistaken, it's actually true. Dirty, who has never been liked, had made the management aware of a rumour. A baseless and defamatory lie. She'd told them my story with the German; or, what she had seen of the story. They didn't believe her: her reputation outweighed the truth. 'A classic case of failing to fit into the corporate culture,' he mused. I shift in my chair; I don't know what to say. 'An angel is protecting me,' I think.

I imagine Dirty splattered on the ground, after falling from an eleventh floor. Her body a mess of guts and blood. The only thing that comes to mind to say is: 'What goes around comes around.' Her sacking is an example to anyone who tries to mess with me. From now on the gardener will do what I say. I receive a message. I feel my phone vibrate against my leg. It must be one of my men.

★

Simon comes to pick me up from the clinic. The gesture is more about possession than a token of affection: he's marking his territory. He barely speaks. He's a ghost. I sling my bag over my shoulder and get on the back of the bike. The tops of the trees shake. The wind wants to disrupt things, tear everything off the face of the earth. He pushes and pushes. It's not a good day for the Ninja. 'Motorbikes are unnatural,' I say. In the countryside, the sky seems infinite. On one side, it stretches to the woods; on the other it sinks behind a ranch; but those aren't its limits, rather it carries them ahead in its path, devouring them.

Simon goes through the gate, waves to the security guard and drives along a straight stretch of road, keeping close to the edge. He pushes down on the accelerator. I hate him. I sink into a spiral of depression. If I get out of this alive, I'll never get on the motorbike again. I swear.

We reach the city and I'm almost spent. The wind has calmed down a bit, or we're protected by the buildings. We go to a bar in a fashionable part of town. Simon chooses a table out on the street so he can keep an eye on his bike. Suddenly two hours have gone by and we've put back three beers each. I go to the bathroom and check my phone: a message from Dirk. Another invitation, another way of seeing things. It's a real joy being many people in one. I adjust my clothes and return to the fray.

Another beer, a plate of papas bravas. I know Simon: he's worried. 'Something's wrong,' I say. He shrugs his shoulders. There's a moment of silence. The traffic is incessant. People come and go. In cars or on foot; they shout when they greet each other. They move. Here, identity is associated with youth.

Simon tells me that yesterday he went to a cocktail party in the Palais de Glace. Someone – a theatrical producer, I think – mistook him for another actor. 'An idiot,' he adds. He undoes a button on his shirt. He rubs his hands together. He looks like he's about to cry. 'He confused me with another actor, can you believe it? He confused me with another actor,' he repeats and gives me a forced smile. The night now has almost no scent. Simon puts a piece of potato in his mouth. He chews and shows his teeth, perfect, square, partly covered by his lips. I guess what's running through his head. Apart from a few exceptions, men are literal. *Have you met the endless traveller on the way to her homeland? She is longing for some confidence, something stable in her hands*, sings Max from the band Vorteilspack. His tender voice surges from the speakers, ripples through the tables, and disappears.

★

The water is tepid, bordering on hot. I gather some in a jug and pour it over Jessica's shoulders. I rinse her. I avoid making eye contact. I don't respond to her; I don't register her gratitude. I know I mustn't encourage any empathy between us; but I still carry out my duties. For example, I monitor the dilation of her pupils. They're two saucers that swallow things up. I also note the redness of her eyes and the blotches on her skin. I dry her gently so as not to cause her skin to peel. Her skin is extremely delicate: every fold is pink. She's enveloped in a strange light, which seems to emanate from her flesh rather than the daylight. When I rub her with the towel she closes her eyes and when I dress her – I have an assistant – she sings, or more accurately she hums, a song she has just made up.

I now inject her. She doesn't complain. She gasps and silently cries. I believe that pain opens up new worlds. I push her to make her walk. 'It's a beautiful day,' I say. We walk through the gardens. The setting is wintry, even though spring supposedly began three days ago. Jessica barely speaks: her morale is really low. She drags her feet. I order her to walk properly. 'I've given my all,' she says. She wants to stop the treatment. I tell her that I have no part in that decision, that she needs to talk to the relevant person. She looks at me as if she didn't know who I was. Immediately, I notice a change in the gardeners' behaviour. All of them, even Dirty's confidant, greet me politely. A dog – an unusual sight – emerges from behind a bush, urinates in a flowerbed and comes towards us. It's a furry and friendly animal. It lies on its back so we can stroke it. I've never really liked animals. We ignore it but it follows us, wagging its tail. All of a sudden, Brodsky sees what's happening and, following an impulse that still isn't clear to me, runs towards us. I ask myself if we're in danger. The dog spots him from a distance, gets agitated and runs away. The gardeners don't understand what's going on. They look at each other, bewildered. They decide it's best to approach us. They all run. The air feels close, as if a storm was about to break and we needed to seek shelter. Our feet are stuck to the ground. We're an unmovable axis, the centre of gravity itself. Jessica grabs my arm. Her eyes are asking me why I've stopped loving her, why I am so indifferent. I have no words to comfort her so I remain silent. We're encircled by a supernatural silence.

The treatment is slowly contaminating Jessica's body; second by second it's destroying her. Brodsky insists that the gardeners are responsible for the security of the gardens. He berates them for failing to do their job properly. He shouts. He's furious. Drops of saliva shoot out of his mouth. His inflamed face defies explanation.

★

This time Dirk pushes the boundaries a little further. 'Let's go to the coast,' he suggests. I love the idea of going to the beach at this time of year. I negotiate a weekend with Simon: like all people, I'm an excellent liar. I am flawlessly duplicitous. I want to clarify that I have my reasons, my man doesn't even bother looking at me. I mount an attack. I don't leave anything to chance. I plan everything down to the smallest detail. I'm sincerely offended when, at this stage of the game, Simon starts to distrust me. It's distressing, a wound in the soul; yet I am hopeful that the trip will heal things.

I am excited about my little trip with Dirk. Like a teenager, I throw myself into our secret romance. I hear him pant over the phone and I feel like I have the world at my feet. I haven't seen the sea for months and I think I've lost the idea of it. I need to see that it's still there. Hear it. Submerge myself completely.

The road is quiet. We move as if in a dream. And this way of relating to things, this understanding of the world, leads us to link two supposedly contradictory ideas: speed and moderation. We pass each other mints and exchange remarks, jokes and an unexpected saying. We breathe in. We are extremely nice to each other.

Dirk, adapted as he is to the customs of this country, asks me to prepare the mate. He's brought everything we need. From the car's airtight cabin I watch the countryside go by: cows, signs, ranches, agricultural machinery, trees. We stop at a service station to stretch our legs. Alongside the smell of petrol I can detect the smell of the sea and it stirs my soul: a feeling of ecstasy takes hold of me. I want to jump with joy.

We arrive at our destination on time. We leave the car parked at an angle and rush into the hotel. We're paranoid, I acknowledge it. We're pursued by the fear of being caught in the act.

Against my expectations, the room is cosy. The bed, which is huge, faces a 40-inch LED TV that Dirk turns on as soon as we settle in. We're on the twelfth floor. Through the window we have a view of the rough sea and, in the distance, on the horizon, flashes of lightning. 'It's going to rain,' Dirk predicts. We lie down to have a rest, but Dirk immediately gets on top of me. I'm lying face up, pushed against the headboard. Dirk thrusts and, between each push, I catch a glimpse of the television. The newsreader speaks without taking a breath: someone has been killed in unclear circumstances. A camera records the moment the victim is hit by a bullet and falls to the ground. They repeat the clip over and over again. I'm obviously obsessed by fat people. I see them everywhere: the woman providing sign language interpretation – from a small box in the corner of the screen – is at least 30 kilos overweight. Dirk's also a heavy man. He's on top of me and I can hardly breathe. But there's something in his lurching that explains it. His rhythm, his obstinate passion, builds a bridge over which my pleasure moves, and this – so intense, so insatiable – makes me amphibious.

★

We're reviewing medical notes in the director's office. We calmly go over the cases one by one and analyse the conclusions. Goldman is sitting on the edge of his seat. He's wearing a pair of blue-rimmed glasses. It seems an insignificant detail but this is carefully planned. This isn't a fashion statement or a nod to the style of the day, nothing of the kind: those glasses, just as I see them now, with their rectangular design, flexible frames, their subtle nose bridge, are ideological. Their functionality and their beauty (above all, their beauty) openly declare on what side of the board the doctor likes to play. An intense smell of coffee floats in the air. Exquisite, roasted beans, Colombian. In front of us, on the desk, a few centimetres from our hands, a pair of empty cups.

Today I arrived at work early. I want to fulfil my duties. I hear the sound of the cleaners. They're as diligent as ants. They carry buckets and brooms, they mop the floor. Every so often, they roar with laughter. On first impression, their lives appear more enjoyable than ours – condemned as we are to administrative monotony – but that's not right, it's a superficial rush to judgement. The truth is they're bored silly. They have no imagination. I can see it in their faces, in their misunderstandings, their shouts and their perfumes.

Three discreet knocks on the door. I'm not surprised when Brodsky comes in. He sees me and raises his eyebrows. It really bothers him that I am alone with Goldman; yet he's polite towards me, greeting me with a cordial smile and immediately getting to the task at hand. 'Mondays are awful,' he remarks. You can smell the milk on his breath, he hasn't digested his breakfast yet. Each word he says is accompanied by a whiff that lingers in the air. Goldman and I exchange a glance and I know he's thinking the same. For the first time, I feel like I'm his partner. Brodsky bites one of his nails, sneezes, asks for a cup of coffee and rubs his eyes; all at the same time. He's crushed by anxiety. He'd like to bite his fingers off. I know him well: I've been watching him all this time.

In the garden the day is just beginning; but in the office it's almost midday. The dust floats in four rays of sunlight. We speak about Jessica. She's not responding to treatment. Goldman is uncomfortable. He moves his legs under the desk, crossing and uncrossing them, and, without meaning to, brushes my legs. 'It can't be possible,' he says. 'More cold and less calories,' he prescribes. He believes the body can be strictly controlled. Meanwhile, Brodsky performs tricks with his incompetence. He's an idiot through and through. 'We have to increase her daily walks,' he suggests. None of them mention the drug being administered to the patient; supposedly the dosage can't be modified. I don't ask questions, that's a given.

I shoot out of Goldman's office. I enter Jessica's room without greeting her, barely looking at her. She's still in bed; so I take advantage of her position to give her an injection. 'The patient is the priority,' I declare before she can say anything. On the bedside table, she has a new hairbrush and a clutch bag. Whoever visited her knows she is a little girl in the body of a woman. When she moves she makes me want to caress and kiss her. She has the softest skin in the world, but I resist, following the protocol. She's in a terrible state: she has dark circles under her eyes and, in addition to the blotches on her skin, she's now jaundiced. I reflect for ten seconds. Then another ten. I should consult with the doctors but an inner strength, my free will, tells me that my judgement is right; that if I don't do this, someone less skilled than I will. With this reassurance, I open the second syringe and pull back the plunger. Jessica watches me. Her eyes brighten. She's not surprised because she has complete faith in me. She breathes in through her nose and stretches out her arm. She extends it as if she were offering up a child or even something more valuable than one's offspring. I search for the vein and find it easily. I palpate it and wait for it to dilate. Then, with extreme care, I select one of the millions of follicles and, at a slight angle, I plunge the needle in. According to the medical literature, the drug will take effect in two minutes.

THE RUNNING MAN

I don't remember if it was a Tuesday or a Wednesday. It was bone-chillingly cold. The sky was far away and overcast. I'd found out that Marilyn Manson had had a rib removed so he could suck his own dick. A stupid thing to remember. Unremarkable. There are no rules about what we forget. Or how we connect one memory to another: that morning and the story about Marilyn Manson, for example.

Wrapped up warm in a thermal tracksuit, I went out for a jog along the coastal path. To my right, the Atlantic Ocean was crashing against the rocks. Far out, half a dozen fishermen were braving the rough sea. None of this has anything to do with training; I'm just setting the scene. That's just how things were. The wind was lashing, pushing me sideways. Before I arrived at the boulevard my legs were starting to feel tired from the uphill slope. The path that leads up to the Magna Carta monument, which has the best views of the area, starts there.

Normally, that's where I meet up with Max Edelmann. Or, more precisely, that's where Max Edelmann waits for me. Every time I run along the coastal path, gasping for air, I spot him in the distance. He's my lighthouse, my goal. He wears a black woollen hat pulled down over his ears. He brought it back from

Vietnam. It was given to him by a lover he met in the Argentinean Embassy. It's an indefensible hat. It even has a sticker of a devil's head on it. However, I have to admit, it suits him. It makes his features look even more refined. The skin on his face is rough and he has light-coloured eyes. With the hat on he looks like a sailor from the battleship Potemkin.

Edelmann arrived seven years ago from a town in Austria. According to him, he has dedicated his life to communication. It's never clear what he means by that. He inhabits that uncertainty; in fact, he exploits it to get what he wants. At first he worked on the cable car, pulling the levers inside a little wooden hut. He looked trustworthy through the window, with those German features of his. Then he worked at the radio station and the most important local paper. From that position, which carries a certain prestige, no one can move him. Whenever he gets the chance, he tells people he's the nephew of the baritone Otto Edelmann. He says it as if he had something to do with the singer's success. He talks about Schubert's Lieder as if he'd sung them himself.

My point is that on the day I'm talking about, Edelmann didn't come running with me. This meant I had to make double the effort. I was out of breath. My legs were tight. When I was running up the hill I heard a ship's horn sound in the distance, then straight away, almost overlapping with it, the siren announcing the second shift in the fish meal factory.

The factory is a building that dates from the late nineteenth century. It's like a monastery, with high walls and barred windows. There, leisure is clandestine. At the end of each shift, those coming out are not the same as those who entered. They've become moles. They have no eyes, their hair is like straw, their skin burns or is forgotten altogether. They're dead tired. Ready for oblivion. It's normal to see them staring at their hands. They don't know what to do with their free time. While they grind fish bones they grind themselves down. They end up becoming the poorest kind of meal.

When I reached the top of the hill I got my second wind. I stopped to give my legs a break. I rubbed my face with my hand, the way a child does. Then, I inspected my surroundings: stone paths, benches, rubbish bins, the ridiculous Magna Carta monument. I wasn't surprised by Edelmann's absence. I knew he had a work commitment, he'd told me so yesterday afternoon.

The break in my run only lasted a minute, enough time to catch a glimpse, out of the corner of my eye, and from up high, of a strip of sea that dredged up an image from the past: I'm fifteen years old, about to enter the water at a beach in Santa Monica, California. I'm wetting my feet at the sea's edge. For hours the sun has been beating down but it is not hot and I suddenly shiver, feeling the most intense cold of my life. It's a memory without purpose, something that emerges from nowhere and evaporates in an instant, but for some unknown reason it stuck in my head. It was a certain climate, an atmosphere.

I continued jogging at a slower pace. The southerly wind persisted. Some gusts targeted the rocks; others created whirlwinds of sand. Without thinking, I turned left and started going downhill through the pine trees. Slowly the scent of the pines began to overpower the sea air; you could say the water lost ground. I took the track that led to the docks. On my right, electric cables and storage sheds; on my left, the pine trees closing ranks, a man in overalls, a pickup truck with its doors open. I registered everything without turning my head. The landscape was part of my field of vision. Periphery: a detail, an ephemeral photo.

When you train you have to ignore your legs. That's what I did that day. That's what I always do. I concentrated on my breathing and the blood pumping through my body. I could have continued down that path without ever flagging but I noticed an open gate and went through it. The wood was the first detour from my routine, but I felt confident. I quickly got used to the uneven ground. The first thing that changed was the light: a cold glare. I ran deep into the trees for two or three kilometres. I skirted the edges of a muddy lake. A seemingly endless expanse of water. A flock of ducks flew low over my head. In that moment I felt my muscles tense and a light contraction in my chest. A strange idea came to me: it is tiredness that alters the landscape, not the other way round. That's what I thought, whimsically: things change when the body decides. A while later, everything was okay again. My heart was beating at its normal rhythm.

Before emerging from the woods, I picked up a trail. As I passed between two cypress trees, I suddenly felt something scratch my face, grazing my skin and leaving a burning sensation. It was an object the size of a fist. I saw how it bounced twice on the ground and then rolled along, coming to a standstill against the root of a tree. I did what I could to soothe the pain, licking my hand and moistening my cheek with saliva. Then I moved cautiously, slowly, towards the thing on the ground, as if it were alive and could hurt me. I nudged it with the tip of my foot, picked it up and sniffed it. It smelt like concentrated urine. It was a fruit, a kind of miniature pomegranate. Its skin had been torn by the fall and a yellow pulp that looked like jelly was seeping out. I didn't think twice. I pulled my arm back and threw the pomegranate as far away as possible. It landed among some branches. Lost forever.

One gate marked the beginning of the wood; another, almost identical one, with worn-out hinges and dark moss covering its bars, marked its end. Abruptly, the wood gave way to an open, rough pasture with a pair of stunted trees in the distance. I was running at exactly the same speed as before, but for some reason I felt the air filled my lungs more efficiently. On my right, in perfect line with the horizon, I could make out a column of black smoke that took the form of a slow-moving, long-eared cat. It spun twice in the air and then faded away. Someone was burning tyres. Or a car. Almost at once, the ground became uneven, a thick clay moulded by the tracks of a tractor. These are ant trails, paths used by only a few people. We use them, but they have no name. Edelmann drives down them in a Renault 4 he bought recently. It's an unreliable car, a piece of junk. The Austrian is often to be seen with the window down, spitting out olive stones. It's his way of keeping himself happy. He goes around grinning from ear to ear, as if life were a party. This is how he saves himself on Sunday afternoons, for example, when everyone else is bored out of their minds. At those moments, there is a touch of wisdom in his thin face: he understands perfectly – and this responds to a natural tendency of his, and not to any process of reflection – that the correct attitude is to be constantly on the move and to always put up a fight, whilst always enjoying yourself. Two strands of his blonde hair flutter in the wind. When he gets into the car, he takes off his black hat. He waves hello to everyone.

I hadn't been here in twenty years or more. I didn't know which way to go. I thought the best thing to do would be to continue in a straight line, without veering off down any side tracks. So that's what I did. The cable car pylons guided me. Thanks to them I knew which way was east, which was all I needed.

I take note of two details. The first: a tree without a single leaf, tough, as if made of stone, part of a clumsy *mise-en-scène*. The second: two birds with shiny black feathers, probably blackbirds. Curved beaks, short wings, puffed-up chests. Warily alert. Their uncertainty infected me, it got into my veins. 'What lies in store for us?', they seemed to be asking. Perching on the edge of a forty-four gallon drum, their heads twitched from side to side: some evil was stalking them; that was clear. The air should have been their refuge – they knew that well – but danger, the vertigo of danger, tied them to the ground. They waited, almost in a trance, their claws gripping the side of the barrel. Ready to flee. I picked up my pace as fast as I could, my heart tearing itself out of my chest. It was time for the last push. My mouth tasted of salt, acetone, rust.

A low privet hedge followed. I crossed over it easily in a running jump. And then, not more than twenty metres away, a hut appeared out of nowhere, like a whim of the Pampas. It was a rectangle of corrugated metal with a gable roof. A cheap building, simple to the eye. To the right an empty pen, a zinc trough; to the left, the grass and the huge plain stretching into the distance. The obstacle gave me an excuse to stop. I was tired, soaked in sweat, at my limit. Any excuse would do. I exhaled. As always, the noises of the countryside, faint but present, took control. They candidly orchestrated the rhythm of things and determined our choices.

I breathed in deeply. I went through a cloud of flies and then immediately came across the swollen body of a dead cow, its legs in the air. Then two more. And another. The last one was lying in the entrance to the hut. Its legs were torn to pieces. Something shook inside of me but I kept going. Inside the hut, I came across another cow, alive this time. I had never seen such a skinny animal. It stared at me and let out a long, deep lowing: a cry that came from a place more ancient than its throat. The cow just about moved its head before giving up. Sprawled out on some tarpaulin with its eyes fixed on me, without seeing me, it was focused on its own internal struggle: the protagonist of a process in which it could not intervene. It lay there, immobile, smelling the air impregnated with urine and dung. An intense physical reaction made me retrace my steps. I left at the same speed as I had come. As I ran, I imagined the cow in the dead of night. It was healthy. It nibbled the tender grass. I arrived home faster than expected and took a hot shower.

The rest of the day I kept myself busy. I changed my sheets, washed my clothes, brought in wood and made a fire in the hearth. Then I sat down in the wicker chair with my feet up. I thought about doing some drawing, which I don't do very often. I keep my pencils and a ream of Fabriano paper, my favourite kind, in the back room. I had trouble finding them. I climbed a small step ladder, feeling around in the dark on the top shelf of a wardrobe. I brought down the wrong box and discovered on opening it an old automatic Webley revolver and a jewellery box holding five bullets. A relic, an ornament. It used to belong to a man who was like a father to me. After a while I found my drawing things. I returned to my chair. I sketched a face with strong features – a version of Beethoven – until it got dark. Almost without thinking, I started to get ready to leave. In a small bag I put everything I needed for my excursion.

As usual the Lada's engine was playing up but I managed to get the car started. There was a strong smell of the sea. I travelled three kilometres along the deserted road. When I spotted the big advertising sign of the Soria farm I slowed down. Twenty metres later I glimpsed the outline of the gate where I had to pull in. I left the car under a casuarina tree and continued on foot. It was unbearably cold. I had come well prepared, wrapped-up, and carried a torch. I shone it on the dead cows and then the corrugated metal hut. In the morning I had arrived there through the wood, which now was the darkest part of the night. I stopped at the entrance to the hut. The cow lay there in agony. This was no tragedy; it didn't demand any attention, the animal was simply completing a biological process, without any drama. I felt a sense of uselessness, which helped me take action. I loaded the gun, held my breath, fired. The cow was struck in the head, but I had only wounded it. I measured the distance better and took aim again, shooting twice. The gunpowder burnt my fingers. I lowered my gun and passed my hand over my face. I barely felt any pain. The cow had fallen on its side. I observed it for a couple of minutes, without trying to reach any conclusion. I picked up the gun and left the hut. I was distracted by an owl, illuminated by the glow of my torch. I felt more than ever that I had to do something, but I didn't know what. I got into my car but it took a while to get it started. As I returned home, in the midst of all that freezing desolation, I realised I was at peace and that from then on, things would begin to change. It was strange and unexpected: a certainty, something lived, a belief that filled me with joy. It was an unprecedented, extraordinary feeling. I hadn't felt anything so intense since my early childhood.

THE NIGHT BEFORE

Open countryside. Four hours after midday. The sun still burns strongly, though it's challenged every so often by toxic gusts of wind, an enemy force. The aroma of grilled meat, seasoned with its faint flavour of fiesta, is still making the mouths of the men water. Some are silently busy with their guns, studying them as if they concealed a secret. Others, lost in thought or distracted, smoke and gaze at the rough line of the horizon. Its only hospitable feature is an enormous, solitary carob tree. The rest of the landscape slowly crushes the spirit. Everything, from the horses' manes to the food, is covered in dust, creating a lack of definition. It is a coarse, dirty-white powder that gets into the hidden folds of matter and weakens it.

In the main tent, Colonel Roca is searching for a word to describe the burning in his chest. He thinks. He strokes his regal beard. After some time, he's distracted by a pair of deep voices tangled in conversation. It's the soldiers. They're making small talk to pass the time. Trivialities. The tallest one, who's wearing a faded jacket, declares that he knows how to drive women crazy with love; he says the key is to look at them firmly, with authority. The other one, who has cauliflower ears and lank, greasy hair, shakes his head in disagreement. When he talks he shouts. His voice is a squawk. He says that no look is that important, and that he doesn't trust anybody. He loses his train of thought, gets tied up in his reasoning, and ends up telling a story about how his brother lost an arm in a fight. A black dog with the muzzle of a wolf barks at the sky, which today is almost cloudless, then rolls over a couple of times and curls up on the ground. Colonel Roca tries to concentrate on his work. He's writing a letter in elegant cursive handwriting. He progresses slowly, very slowly. He's so meticulous it's exasperating. The sound of his pen scratching against the paper fades into the drowsy afternoon.

He keeps his head down, focused on his work, until he realises there's a man waiting at the entrance to the tent, standing at attention. The man is tall, with square shoulders; he has a thick moustache and a sly expression on his face. His eyes are two dark lines. His uniform still tries to keep up a pretence of elegance. For a short time, no more than ten seconds, Roca doesn't recognise his assistant of over three years. Then he raises his head and gestures to him.

'What do you want?' he asks curtly.

The soldier is slow to respond. He breathes in deeply. He knows hesitating isn't the correct thing to do, but that's what he does. He can't find the right way of communicating the message to his superior. Roca waits. An imperceptible tremor brings his lips to life and his face changes, as if it were folding in on itself. He looks at his assistant without blinking. He seems to despise him.

The soldier says:

'Excuse me, Colonel… There's been an Indian waiting by the guard post for a while now. She's insisting on talking to you. She says she's the sister of Yanquetruz.

Chief Yanquetruz'.

Roca abruptly rises to his feet. He furrows his brow. There's a cloud surrounding him, deciding his actions.

'Sending a woman to negotiate... Have they no shame?'

★

The woman is thickset, with the gaze of someone used to arid landscapes, vast distances, the open sky. Two wrinkles frame her mouth. Her hair, which is long, which is dark, which is almost another body enveloping her body, casts her masculine face into shadow. She has a bad-tempered look about her, even though she's patient and used to waiting, no matter for how long. She understands and respects the world she knows. Right now she is worried about words. She doesn't trust the truthfulness of a language that isn't hers. There are five people in the tent, but she's looking directly at Roca. He looks as if he was born to read the endless pile of papers they have just brought him.

The woman barely moves. She is swaying slightly, and every so often she scratches at the base of her skull. She can feel the tracks of the lice on her skin and the suspicion of the soldiers. The woman has no name. La Mala, they say when they refer to her. The Evil Woman. Colonel Roca looks up but he doesn't get to his feet. He's sitting on a wicker chair.

'What do you want?' he asks her.

La Mala thinks for a few seconds, pausing as if she'd forgotten the reason she's come to see the white man.

Then she speaks. Her voice is so abrasive the soldiers around her feel a strange sense of uneasiness. A disquiet they will never speak of and prefer to forget as soon as possible.

La Mala doesn't speak good Spanish, but she tries to make herself understood. She mentions her brother. 'Yanquetruz, Chief Yanquetruz,' she says. She tells them about the smoke that is the first sign of light around a campfire; about the erratic nature of change; about the comings and goings of her people; about the deep disregard for what she calls, without realising it, the body of the earth. 'The body of the earth,' she says, adding, 'and the body of things.'

Then she speaks about the arbitrary design of the days. She tells them – as best as she can, mounted on words that are a herd of fleeing horses – about the wild twists and turns of life that raise dust even at the moment of death. The soldiers watch her indifferently. They don't care what this woman might say. Only Colonel Roca seems concerned enough to try and understand. Taking advantage of a brief pause, he asks:

'What are you trying to tell me?'

La Mala then turns her head and points at the landscape as if it were an ally. She says something they don't understand, a bundle of sounds that zigzag between the men as if she had burped. La Mala rubs her mouth with the side of her hand. She wishes she could correct her mistake: she has spoken in the wrong language and she fears the consequences. She believes her voice knows something that she herself is unaware of.

As soon as the air fills her throat, she asks Colonel Roca for space. Space for each nation to know their own history, develop their own traditions, and erect their own standing stones without destroying those of the others. 'We cannot be any other way,' La Mala says, 'We cannot, however much the knife cuts or the fire burns. You can see the wound in the other's chest but you cannot feel their pain.'

Colonel Roca listens attentively, and senses the need to take a position. He runs his tongue along his teeth. Clenches his fist.

'I promise to give you an answer. Tomorrow, before midday, you'll know what I think,' he says, and brings the interview to an end.

★

Three hours before sunrise. Colonel Roca sits upright in his camp bed. He smooths his hair with one hand and stands up. While he gets dressed he looks at the shape left by his body in the sheets. He coughs. An excess of phlegm troubles his throat. He thinks about spitting but grimaces instead: after such a poor night's sleep, he tries to recover his composure.

Now he is walking beneath a sky that, for the first time in his life, seems eternal. 'It's chilly,' he says. Suddenly the whole countryside rushes over him with the noises of the fading night. A cricket, the faraway sound of the horses, the wind blowing against the leaves. His insomnia is like a sting to the forehead. He can't stop thinking about La Mala. 'Damn woman,' he grumbles. 'Lecturing me about space.'

Colonel Roca would like to smoke. He sticks a blade of grass between his teeth and chews it. Walking with slow steps, he studies the thud of his boots against the ground. He believes the national project is imbued in his very blood, it is the power that enables him to order someone's throat to be cut. To leave no room for doubt: it is certainty itself. It is as clear as day, as clear as the water that fills the rivers.

But Roca, in that moment, is thinking about the Indian, about her abrasive voice saying what she said. And this man, who has not yet fulfilled his destiny, despises himself for holding on so keenly to the echo of some words he didn't even need to hear.

Colonel Roca doesn't want to listen to the Indian any more than he wants to listen to his uncertainties. 'There are matters for which there is no alternative,' he says. His face darkens with rage.

'Why do they put these stupid ideas in my head?' he shouts without realising.

A soldier hears, glances at the Colonel and then retreats back into the darkness. Another does the same. Later, they will speak about the incident.

★

The day breaks serenely. A flock of birds flies low over the camp. The men gather around the fire, their expressions stern. A solid bank of cloud is advancing from the south. The rain, they all know, will come in the afternoon.

Colonel Roca is wearing a new uniform. Its gold buttons gleam. He looks up and realises his appearance contradicts the surroundings. He folds his lips into a smile, thinking that the destiny of the fatherland requires determination and courage. He makes a remark in a low voice, but no one catches it. His hand, hardened by military rigour, clasps his only response: the cold testimony of the sword.

THE TERRACE

1

It was simple: at 10.30 a.m. we used to go and smoke on the terrace. Although really it was less a terrace than a large, tiled roof. We'd light one cigarette after another, observing the neighbourhood from the stratosphere: trees, houses, thousands of antennae, the odd cloud. That watchtower of ours had a special energy. The air was rough and constant, like the wind which crests the Andes. When it brushed your face it left a mark; your cheeks taut. The terrace must have been on the fifth floor, or at most the sixth, but it was high enough to give you vertigo. Nothing less than a roof on the edge of infinity. Standing on one of the ledges, your heels resting on the tiles and your toes in mid-air was an extreme sport. The challenge had an uncertain smell, a mix of sweat and cement. Being up there with your pals, escaping from daily life, was the best way to deal with the world.

We found that place by chance. One Wednesday in March. Freytas, the maths teacher, came into the classroom. She was like a stork: egg-shaped skull, extremely long neck. She lived on Calle Virrey Cevallos, looked after her mother and proved theorems. That's what is known, what is said about her. That day, Freytas told us her throat hurt. You could tell she was ill. She probably had a fever. She stared at the window frame and waited for us to do something. It was unbelievable that she thought we'd help her, but she was genuine. And this sincere gesture – a weakness, in our eyes – made her the perfect victim and, at the same time, endeared her to us: the woman was desperate and was asking for help from her executioners. This may be a common occurrence in other settings but in a secondary school it's unusual. Abadi beat me to it. He stood up and offered her a cup of tea. She accepted. Abadi was as fast as lightning; he was in and out of the kitchenette in a second. He returned with a steaming cup in his hands and a set of keys in his pocket. He'd stolen them from the office. 'They're the keys to the terrace,' he whispered.

The next day, we organised our first outing. The terrace quickly became a bad habit. We had discovered the school's degree zero. Passing through a corrugated iron door we found paradise: privacy, tobacco, open air. It was a secret shared between four of us: Gabito, Mateos, Abadi and me. We had the good fortune of the cautious. We would escape during our breaks and free periods. Knowing our discovery was going to be short-lived, we tried to enjoy every moment. We bought a small bottle of Bols and hid it behind the air vent, but we barely drank the gin. It tasted disgusting but we thought that, in this place, it was important to have. Transgression, we quickly realised, ruled the scene. There were a few ingredients that were essential. Wetting your lips with alcohol was an attitude, a gesture which, whatever the eventualities, would show us which things to be faithful to, and which not. Months went by without incident.

The only person who noticed our absence was that idiot Benazar. In a moment of weakness, I told him about the terrace. I thought I was doing him a favour. He was an only child, pale and with terrible skin, and letting him in on a secret seemed like a necessary way of boosting his self-esteem.

I made a mistake, I admit it. I'm the kind of person who trips over the same stone twice. One morning he asked me if I'd show him the terrace. I turned away, avoiding the question. Benazar didn't say anything but made a gesture with his eyes – opening and closing them in slow motion – which was proof that he wouldn't let it go.

May arrived and brought with it a cold breeze, but we put up with it just fine. There was one splendid morning when the sun peeked out just enough to make the world seem promising. We were on the terrace and we'd taken our shoes off. We were talking about ourselves as if we were other people, carefree and detached. Mateos was lying on his back, looking at the sky. His large eyes were wide open. The shadow of a beard covered his chin. The four of us were as still as deer, barely disturbed by an intermittent breeze. One step away from being immortal. If I'd known then that scene would become one of my memories, I'd have tried to retain more of its details. Those were simple days. Pleasures were quick to leave a mark.

Benazar lurked in the shadows. He conducted himself perfectly, as meticulous as a watchmaker. He didn't do it directly, but used a third party. With us he was friendly but distant. He made it clear he could survive on his own. He was totally focused on his actions: resentment fed his spirit. There was nothing of the unpleasant aftertaste of innocence left in him. At break times he stood staring blankly into the distance, with his evil little smile on his face.

He chose well. He spoke to Britos, a girl who was always scared. The world, to her, was a place where everyone had to pay, whether or not they made mistakes. Her mouth was as soft as a frayed thread. She was strict in her habits: in the second break she would always buy two sandwiches and eat them quickly, without enjoying them. During one free period Benazar approached her and casually told her about the terrace. He knew no one likes tell-tales so he chose to frame the story as a confession. He said he was part of a group that went up to the terrace to take drugs. They'd peer into the abyss, spitting, risking their lives. He told her nothing less than the old story of young death. Benazar didn't have time to savour the wait: the following day the information was public. Britos had told her mother, who suffered from severe anxiety, and she'd gone to the school authorities with the story.

They slammed open the door to the terrace. We had cigarettes in our mouths. First came the fat caretaker; two steps behind, the headteacher, the director of studies and one of the prefects. Out of fright, I raised my arm in a kind of Nazi salute and showered them with insults. 'Fuck you, you fucking arseholes,' I shouted. That was my downfall: they accused me of being the instigator, intellectual author and perpetrator of the crime. There was no discussion. I was immediately expelled.

Gabito went with me. Our criminal records seemed to be exact copies of each other, but they were based on a biased viewpoint. Papers always lie. Besides, the school we attended was Lutheran; the pastor and the board of governors had a pessimistic vision of freedom. 'Dead dogs don't bite,' the headteacher must have thought as he threw us out. Abadi and Mateos had a narrow escape. They weren't as tainted as we were. Benazar didn't even bother to make up an excuse. His face and stupid little voice were his get out of jail free card.

2

It wasn't until a week later, once all the fuss had died down, that it hit me. My parents weren't talking to me and my ten-year-old sister was giving me disapproving looks. Suddenly, I'd become suspicious, almost a criminal; I felt like someone else in my own body. No school would let me enter even the entrance hall. The same thing happened to Gabito. We would speak for hours on the phone to try and make ourselves feel better but there was no point, nothing worked. We were rotten and crazy, sick.

I spent the whole day lying in bed. I watched telly, played solitaire, read comics. I'd fallen down a bottomless pit. My karma was shit, a magnet for disaster. I took one false step after another. One morning at the crack of dawn I woke up dying of thirst. I went to the kitchen to get a glass of water and took the living room table with me. Result: a broken little toe. On another occasion, one Saturday morning, I went out to buy some crackers. My old man loves them. I walked the three blocks to the bakery without incident, but as I was coming back the same way, a dog sunk its teeth into my leg. It was a sudden attack. They had to give me seven stitches in A&E. Unheard of for the size of the creature. Its mouth was smaller than my fist.

All this reminded me of the saying: all bad things come in threes, and I took extreme precautions. I wanted to soften the blow of the final misfortune. How naïve of me: I had no chance. I got a bad case of shingles and the pain drove me crazy until my aunt suggested a treatment with Indian ink. It left me weak, submerged in a vague melancholy. As my parents watched me languish, something changed. They went from being angry to feeling sorry for me.

While I waited for any college to be kind enough to let me in, I started helping out some guy called Patta who delivered noodles in a van. I wasn't exactly having a bad time, but I missed the lost paradise. When Gabito and I got into vocational college I felt as if I could touch the sky. I thought things were finally going in the right direction. At that time my old man was going on a work trip to New York and he was really excited. After dinner he would show us the historic sites in Manhattan on a map that was falling to pieces. I couldn't contain myself. It was as if he were speaking to me about the path of good fortune to which I had just returned. The effects of the past were coming to an end. I would be left with a scar, nothing else.

The admissions interview was with the headteacher, who called himself Dr Laciar. When I saw him for the first time I was startled. He was two guys in one. He had a small, jangly head stuck onto a body that had thickened with age. His way of speaking reinforced this contrast. He gave me such a warm welcome I distrusted him.

We started one freezing Monday. Gabito and I sat in the only available seats, in the front row by the window.

If we looked to our left we saw a concrete playground that could have easily been Siberia, and to our right were teenagers with sharp, waspish faces. At first glance they all looked the same: greasy hair, blank stares, skin raw with spots. We heard words that referred to us: whiteys, stupid, fags, choir boys. They were ghosts. As we sat there in silence, we felt like they were biting our necks with their eyes. They didn't waste any time. The bullying started at the first break. Gabito looked up, pleading for help from the heavens. Instantly we knew it was going to be worse than we'd imagined. Two weeks later our nerves were destroyed.

In our class there were nineteen guys and three girls who always hung around together. They were survivors in a hostile world. They fed off the living, they knew that cannibalism was their only option. Whenever they appeared things inevitably got worse. They had an amazing talent to incite the torturers. When the girls laid their eyes on you it was trial by fire. In my dreams, and also in Gabito's, their voices were bitter syrup. They cackled. They watched each other the whole time. Every gesture, every movement of their hands, even the trembling of their eyelids was carefully planned out. Their movements mirrored each other. They were enemies but they knew that together they would create the spear to kill the dragon. They took it in turns to have sex with the leader. Patient and salacious. They played with boys as if they were plasticine. Three tyrants. Among the guys their scent was famous; their kisses left them breathless. That's how they took revenge. They demonstrated the extent of the school's absurdity, a machine that used you and then spat you out.

Ascárate was the leader. Evil followed in his wake. He had yellow, crooked teeth. Like every one of his kind he was very gregarious. His voice had a military ring to it. At all times he moved with certainty. Once, he and his friends caught me by surprise in the playground. They wanted to paint my face with a marker pen. In the struggle I lost a shoe. I watched as they lobbed it away. It landed on the roof of an adjacent house. This wasn't an isolated incident. Every day we had to put up with the effects of his poison. We understood that the important thing wasn't to resist but to change our attitude. Move from the zone of vulnerability to that of respect. We wanted to change our personalities. It was about nothing less than survival. Without any decent role model, I thought about my father. He should be the example to follow. As soon as I woke up and before I even got out of bed I would work on my character. We started with the easiest thing, changing our look. I got hold of a pair of black skinny jeans; Gabito, always radical, went for steel-capped Doc Martens. We knew there'd be no sudden miracle but things did change a bit. Just like martyrs, we based our hope on any old nonsense. We were on the right path.

3

A month later, one midday in October, a group of us from school went out. Everyone was there: Ascárate, his stupid lackeys, the girls, and us. The clouds were low in the sky. You could hear the sound of buses passing on the main road. Spring weighed heavily in the air, like resin.

The tension in the scene was completely controlled by the girls. They to-and-froed, whispering and giggling. They were weaving a bigger plot in which we only played minor roles. Every so often they looked at us to remind us that our wellbeing depended on them. We were hanging by a thread. Gabito was biting his nails, dragging his feet as if he had been condemned to death. There was an imbalance of power that weighed on our shoulders like an extra force of gravity. When we got to Beiró we were breathless. We were moving at one frequency, the world at another.

Ascárate signalled to us and we stopped. He imitated a cowboy, shooting a brief glance. He suggested we go to the news-stand in the station. We agreed, some of us happy, others simply resigned. The girls started to prepare the scene for the sacrifice. It was obvious something was coming. They linked arms with Gabito and asked if he was a virgin. The poor kid knew that there was no valid answer to that question. Everything, including the sound of his voice, was playing against him. He turned his head for a second and I saw his desperation. The sun ricocheted off the tiles and its rays dispersed through the neighbourhood. It was 1.11 p.m. I managed to catch a glimpse of the clock in the pharmacy. We were walking towards the outskirts of town.

The event was triggered by two things. One was Ascárate's attitude. He turned his head towards us and nodded. It was an imperceptible gesture, a minuscule sign. He had established a mandate and, at the same time, offered emancipation. The other was the sound of a door closing, a casual occurrence, which made us face up to what was immediately before us. Those two facts, independent yet connected, left us no alternative. I was about to agree to do it, but Gabito had already obeyed.

He was a couple of metres ahead of the group, gazing at a skinny dog that had appeared out of nowhere, a filthy animal that was focusing all its energy on staying upright. They watched each other for a few seconds. The creature didn't have time to sense it was in danger. It was calm, almost absent. Gabito took a few steps backwards and, after pausing for a second, gave it a brutal kick to the head. For two seconds things stood still. Then, through the air came a sound of bones breaking. The dog rolled over and fell dead. It was something outside of time. A tragedy, a real tragedy. Gabito walked confidently back towards us. Something had changed in him. His eyes were like those of an old man, heavy with exhaustion, yet his mouth – the same as always, the mouth of the child he was – had widened into a smile. He pointed to his boots. 'They're steel-capped,' he said. And that midday, the metallic sound of his voice resonated with the irrefutable weight of the truth.

FIRE

Memory tends to distort things. Yet I could swear that for years when I was a kid, I had the same dream over and over again. The experience was traumatic; when night fell, I would despair. The story that tormented me so is still very present today. The scene takes place in a room with high ceilings. I am asleep in a single bed. A wool blanket presses me down against the mattress. I can't move much. I know that my room is the tenth one in a mansion otherwise unknown to me. I am alone, completely alone. It's freezing cold outside. Suddenly, something, I don't know what, causes a fire that without warning goes from harmless to fierce. Everything burns: the walls, the bed, my whole body. I am burning. The flames are burning me alive but I don't wake up. In the dream, I remain unconscious. The fire engulfs me. I feel my organs collapsing, my skin degrading to nothing. The scene remains forever untouched in my head. That image, in fact, changed my gaze. My relationship with the world is rooted in those burns, those marks invisible on my skin but deeply engraved on my brain. They are the starting point from which I interpret everything.

Last year I attended a workshop on public education that took place in the University of La Plata. It was intense: four six-hour long days. All of us taking part thought that the most practical thing was to stay in the same city. We got a discount at the Toledo Hotel, a small place across from the Alberti park. The rooms are spotless and stuck in the 1970s: lots of tongue and groove timber panelling, fake leather, lino. It's cheap and has a restaurant with bar meals that only opens at lunch time. From the first day of the course, a colleague caught my attention. He was evasive, insipid. He must have been in his sixties. He didn't open his mouth once during the classes. He sat on the same chair at the back of the room every day. He would stare at the speaker, squinting his eyes the way short-sighted people do as if it helped them to reduce distances. Every now and then he would nod, and mumble something to emphasise his agreement. He was strong, with short but toned limbs. His movements spoke of resolution. His name was Mosches. On the second day, during one of the breaks, I stepped out into the street to get some fresh air and found him smoking in the shade of a white cedar. Out of sheer curiosity, I went over and started chatting to him. He was from La Plata himself but lived in Dolores. When I had him directly in front of me, I made out something that − inexplicably − I had overlooked before: on his neck he had a burn mark in the shape of a horseshoe. The skin seemed to have lost its elasticity and looked shrivelled; however, it was the colour of the folds that made the greatest impression.

It's always the same with me: I go on a trip and I withdraw, I don't socialise. I struggle with this trait of mine every now and then, but I must admit it's the one that makes me the happiest. Since I know myself,

I always carry crime novels with me and as soon as I see the opportunity, I sneak away from the meetings to throw myself on the bed and read. In La Plata, for instance, I spent many hours hooked by *Savage Night* by Jim Thompson. A unique pleasure. That's why during the farewell dinner I was looking for the right moment when I could sneak away without offending anyone. The organisers – it has to be said – had excelled themselves in all things academic, but were also exemplary when it came to the food. That night we drank a full-bodied tempranillo and ate spinach cannelloni. When it came to the coffee and the after-dinner talk we were drowsy due to the work our digestive systems were doing, but gregarious behaviour won over everything else. Most people wanted to continue the evening in a bar on 42nd street. At that moment, I made up an excuse, said farewell with a smile and returned to my hotel. As was to be expected, Mosches came along with me. We walked in silence for a couple of blocks. Then we said something or other about the brisk wind, the grid design, the joy of getting lost in a city. We reached our destination without noticing. One of the most beautiful spaces at the Toledo is its fully glazed lounge. From there, you can see a path leading deep into the park. It's the ideal spot for a nightcap. That's how Mosches, who was kind enough to invite me, understood it in any case. We ordered local whisky. He opened up only with the second glass. He said I seemed trustworthy to him, empathetic. I didn't discourage him. I wanted to hear his story. He had joined the Montoneros at the age of seventeen. He'd fallen into militancy, but his commitment took over immediately. He had a precocious relationship with weapons: when he was seven, he used to go hunting partridges with his father.

For this reason, he was able to revel in the gun that a friend – Emilio Maza – placed in his hands. Time added trust and responsibility to his audacity; two virtues which brought him a certain reputation. He was there at Ezeiza airport to receive Perón with a single aim: to be the General's back. Then it all went wrong. What was left was history, and the anecdote.

One day he married a fellow militant. Exactly a year later, on a very quiet Sunday, he was entertaining himself cleaning guns. He was in his little back yard, under a vine. Back then, he lived in La Plata, in the same city where he was now telling me this story. Suddenly – because guns are the devil's work, as Mosches put it – a bullet was fired from a Ballester-Molina that had a very sensitive trigger. The unthinkable happened: it went straight into his wife's head, obliterating it, leaving her dying in a puddle of blood. In desperation, he put her over his shoulder and carried her out into the street. The neighbours witnessed the scene and didn't hesitate: the police were called. Mosches went back inside and wrapped the body in a sheet. He stopped to think for a moment. He was in a bunker; he had no choice whatsoever. He kicked over a table and waited for them to come in. The exchange of bullets was brief and baffling. Mosches got lucky and hit a corporal, who passed away two weeks later. Then, he escaped over the rooftops. He went into hiding but bad luck started to follow him around. A month after the incident, he got caught in a raid. He spent a decade in the Devoto jail, before being set free in an amnesty.

We both remained silent. A short while later, the sound of the hotel elevator cut through the tension. Mosches raised his head and sniffed the air like an animal. I'm not sure where I got the courage from to ask more questions. I was intrigued by that mark on his neck, the one that looked like a burn. He drank the dregs of his whisky and said, in a husky voice, that when he was ten he fell ill and got herpes. First it looked like an allergy but after a fortnight blisters appeared. He spent over two years trying to fight it off. Herpes is a tough disease, he commented, it damages the skin, leaves horrid scars. He explained that it is a viral infection. Not bacterial, but viral, he said. I listened to him carefully and respectfully; yet in all honesty, I know nothing about such things, which meant that his elucidation was completely meaningless to me.

THE COMPLEXITIES OF MATTER

Maggie was just thinking how well things were going for her when she heard the explosion and the screams. She was lying on the bed, facing the ceiling, boots on. It was exactly 3.23 p.m. Her state of mind was like she was dreaming but with her eyes wide open. She was nibbling at a bit of tangerine pith. She'd kept it between her teeth since lunch. The commotion threw her deep into the world. In two leaps, she was by the window. She opened one of the panes and got half of her body out. She looked down in a reflex action and saw a cat between two buckets. The creature stared at her as if she owed it something. The smell of burning merged with the acid tang of the sea. She stretched her neck out as far as she could and made out a rectangle on Calle Camusso, a group of people running, and a badly parked F100 van with an open door. In the background, a column of smoke cancelled the horizon. Two skinny eucalyptus provided the contrast.

A month and three days had passed since Maggie's birthday. Her skin was coppery and she was swift as an impala. She flew down the stairs and into the street. She ran into Barone's wife who was holding one of the twin girls in her arms. Maggie wanted to know what had happened. The woman shrugged her shoulders and said nothing. Then, with her free hand, she pointed towards a Gilera 200 moped. These idiots keep waking my baby up, she said.

Maggie reached the corner. Her awareness registered the pressure of her boots against the broken glass scattered on the ground. A cloud of dust affected her vision, everyone's. People were automatically covering their faces with their hands. No one could make sense of what had happened. Outside the grocery store an improvised assembly upheld the official version: there'd been an explosion in the Materia soap factory. The boiler. They mentioned the boiler. At that moment, the firefighters and ambulance arrived. The number of curious onlookers was growing; most of them were teenagers. The information was confusing but was spreading quickly. There was already talk of casualties, fatalities even. The column of smoke soon dissipated, it occupied a smaller space in the sky. Maggie had been living in Mar del Plata for two years now. She had managed to establish a rhythm for her life. The question of distances was sorted: she could reach the sea in fifteen minutes on her bike.

★

Nothing planned. Maggie's exodus had been decided from one moment to the next. She'd spent her life in the suburbs of Bogotá. Together with her mother and sister – they were both called Sandra – they rented a tiny apartment. It was a corridor with a single window. The owner, whose surname was Durán, weighed

160 kilos and injected himself with insulin. He was a grouch. Every month when he came to get the rent, he complained. He said they didn't know how to look after the place. This is filthy, he'd groan. They laughed at him but gradually his obsession got to them. They set up a cleaning schedule. Wednesdays was Maggie's turn. On the second week of January, when she moved the sofa to mop the floor, a bug crawled up her arm. She didn't notice. A while later, when she felt something creeping down her back, it was too late: she'd been bitten in her armpit. At first, it was just a red dot. After half an hour, things got worse: her lymph nodes swelled up, her left arm was sore, and she felt nauseous.

They rushed to the hospital. It was a delicate situation: she'd encountered an invasive insect. They told her that it had come in a shipment from the Czech Republic. That week alone there had been five cases just like hers. She was hospitalised for two days. The incident – exaggerated from the outset – did not lead to any serious consequences. Sandra, her mother, was by her side at all times. The two of them spoke to the point of exhaustion. The hospitalization had brought their routine to a halt. Among other things, Sandra told her about Juan Esteban, a distant cousin. He was three years older than Maggie and had found religious enlightenment; he attended the Universal Church. Then he'd fallen in love with a Peruvian woman and had migrated to Argentina.

'To Argentina?'

'He was obsessed with that country.'

Maggie wanted to know more, but Sandra was no longer making sense. Juan Esteban and Argentina, Maggie thought: that combination was the embodiment of desire. For her the message was loud and clear. In two months she had sorted out her travels. She got in touch with her cousin – someone gave her his email address – and borrowed money for the ticket. She arrived in Buenos Aires and felt the buildings were collapsing on her. The city was another corridor in her life. She took a taxi to San Telmo and got off at the corner of Chile and Balcarce. She saw a grocery store identical to the one in front of her house in Bogotá. She paid what the meter showed and thought about coincidences. Since she was a little girl, she'd associated them with good fortune.

★

When she learnt that her cousin did not live in Buenos Aires, her trip had already been organised. I'm going anyway, she said to herself. Juan Esteban was staying in Aguas Verdes, a small coastal town on the Atlantic. The first thing Maggie did when she arrived in Argentina was to call him. She said that as soon as she sorted herself out, she'd come and see him. He replied he'd wait for her with his arms wide open, but his voice expressed the opposite. Maggie knew that Juan Esteban worked in the construction industry and that his wife was the jealous type. She foresaw confrontations. However, she was not discouraged by the prediction, but rather spurred on.

In Buenos Aires, she had a single reference to go by: the hostel on Calle Chile. Someone, another Colombian, an acquaintance of an acquaintance, had spent some time there. Ema Gulli, the person in charge, felt an immediate affinity with Maggie and let her have the best room. It was on the top floor. It was quite an ample space with two doors. One led to the stairs that went down to the street; the other, to a neglected rooftop. Maggie was happy there for a while. She would sit on an old sun lounger and stare at the sky, drinking litres and litres of tonic water.

★

One of the advantages of this place was her independence. This is why Maggie felt comfortable breaking the house rules. One night, she brought home a portable cooker and a small gas cylinder. At first, she used it just to warm things up, but as she gained confidence, she started cooking with it: tapioca stew, egg arepas, criollo-style steaks. She was a cashier in a supermarket. She woke up at six every morning with the feeling she hadn't slept at all. At night she would pee with her eyes closed so as to avoid waking up fully. Since there was usually not much water, she avoided taking showers. When she returned from the bathroom to her room, she'd usually cross paths with two other residents whom she gracefully dodged. For breakfast she had oatcakes and coffee. Then she headed to work. She had to walk one block; it took her six minutes. She paid close attention to her feet, her knees and the striking variety of the world. But behind the till, life was different. Radically so. It was repetitive, monotonous: the same customers, the same turn around the sun. The coming and going of people she gazed at obliquely was automatic, embodying a lack of purpose. Those details, nonetheless, were the basis of her well-being.

★

One morning she woke up with a toothache. She went to a dental clinic that was on Calle Tacuarí. She was seen by a really tall man – almost six and a half feet – who was fifteen years her senior. He was so rough with the dental explorer that he hurt her gums. The following day, they began a relationship which endured no time at all. On their final encounter they spent the entire time in Maggie's room. She cooked meat with vegetables. Then they lay down in her narrow bed. While they were making love Maggie got unwontedly distracted. She became fixated by the pattern of a curtain she'd put up a week earlier. The dentist left at 7 p.m. and she made the most of her solitude: she went out to the rooftop with her tonic water. She sat on the lounger and re-read a letter from her mother. She was sharing trivialities: her cousin Duilio had bought himself a Chevrolet, one of the walls was peeling, the tap water seemed dirty. Maggie waited for the night to arrive up on the rooftop and achieved something extraordinary: with what she had to hand, she constructed a sense of joyous intimacy.

★

There was a second explosion. Then, silence. A gelid silence, like in the opera. Right away, a wall came crumbling down. People's first reaction was to escape, even the firefighters ran for their lives. Trenches were improvised. Maggie, for instance, stumbled upon an old Bedford truck and she thought the back wheel – huge, absurdly so – made the perfect sheltering space. The afternoon breeze ricocheted against her dry hair. And the brutal slovenliness of the street suddenly contrasted with the neatness of the sky. In one corner, there was a tiny moon in broad daylight. Maggie shared her shelter with two other people: a man wearing glasses and a dishevelled young lad in bermuda shorts. Nothing to be said. They were staring at the soap factory with their mouths wide open, obeying the eternal desire of witnesses: to fall in love with the immediate truth.

The onlookers gradually emerged. Maggie had a privileged view of the scene. She saw six firefighters go through the factory's main entrance. They were a team and had experience, there was no doubt about that. This trait, disagreeable though it may be, made them insensitive. With utter lack of care, they pulled out five victims in twenty minutes; one of them in a black bag. A rumour quickly went round that it was the owner's son. An image stayed with Maggie: an arm hanging down from beneath a sheet. It was a loose, bodyless thing. Soon enough that shape mutated in her brain. It became a state of mind – a stupor, a vague feeling of unease – that remained with her all day. The rumours turned out to be correct: the boiler had exploded. The official version was issued by a policeman. He provided some technical details and got muddled up with the particulars. People began to disperse. Maggie, alert, glanced at her mobile phone and headed home as if she had something urgent to do.

★

One morning in September she walked away from the hostel on Calle Chile. She was wearing her hair down and a hoop pierced her right nostril. She'd told Ema Gulli that a relative had found her work on the coast. Lying came naturally to her, not a single word too many. Before leaving the place, she gave Ema a tiny elephant made of china. She suggested she should tie a banknote to its trunk for luck. Then she made a gesture with her hand, as if wanting to take hold of the world, and added that it was an ornament she'd had since she was a little girl. The truth is she'd just stolen it, along with a wad of notes, from a certain Justin, with whom she'd been involved in recent months. Justin was trusting despite his background: he'd arrived a year before from Lesotho and earned a living selling goods on the street.

Maggie gave Ema a big farewell hug. She'd got bored of working in the supermarket. Her decision to change paths had been swift. As a matter of fact, it was a process made up of different stages, though to her this succession had gone unnoticed. She had taken shelter on the surface of her own self, with the focus set on what there was to come. As she walked away, she felt nostalgic, as if this departure – in contrast with the previous ones – would carry decisive consequences. The feeling she had was more confusing, but just as intense as the one she felt when she left Bogotá. Before getting on the bus, Maggie bought two packs of Granix cookies. As soon as the bus had left the city boundaries, she began to swallow one cookie after the other. She saw the industrial grid of the suburbs, and soon after, the vastness of the plains. The landscape unfolded in front of her meaninglessly. Before arriving at the town of Dolores, a fine drizzle misted the tarmac, the trees and the cows. The bus continued at its pace regardless, its sidelights on. The sound of the engine and the unvarying road plunged Maggie into a dreamless slumber.

★

The Peruvian woman was taller than her husband, and looked at him out of the corner of her eye as if he were a flaw in her field of vision. They were both actively religious and attended a church that was next to a supermarket selling DIY products. They prayed many times a day and at any opportunity. They consulted God about everything. They also watched a lot of television. They had dinner early and went to bed before eleven. Maggie stayed at that house for three weeks. She'd go for endless strolls in the woods and along the beach. One morning, she went to the sea and filled a bag with clams. She made a tortilla with them which no one cared to try. Juan Esteban said to her that he and his wife had sensitive stomachs; their diet consisted mostly of steamed vegetables.

In Aguas Verdes there was no shelter for Maggie: the sea was icy, people were indifferent, the Peruvian woman unreceptive. Maggie embodied a threat to her world, that was clear from the outset. Nevertheless, the Peruvian did not go for direct confrontation. She kept her rivalry muted. That was plenty. The day came when Maggie urgently wanted to leave. A conscript offered to take her to Mar del Plata. They travelled in an army truck and stopped at an eatery by the road where they ate grilled offal and shot the breeze. The sun filtered through the branches, bounced among the weeds and ended up somewhere in a corner of the field. It was the first time she'd felt such strong nostalgia. She wished she'd never left her home country.

★

In Mar del Plata, Maggie changed. In eight months, she'd become a different person. Her eyes took on a new shape. She had straightened her posture: she was now two centimetres taller. She jumped from one job to another until she found a position as a receptionist in an eye clinic. It wasn't too challenging and they were quite flexible with her hours. Almost every morning, in the staff room shared by doctors and admin people, she drank coffee from a big mug. It was then, on one such nondescript day, that her perspective shifted: the things that before went unnoticed suddenly began to catch her attention. She moved slowly in a sluggish, empty city. Before her first winter there, she met a patient who was from Chapadmalal, a guy who played covers of Joan Manuel Serrat in seedy bars. His surname was Brailovsky; his friends called him the Russian. He was two years younger than her and had a three-year old son that came to stay with him at the weekends. Brailovsky asked her out a couple of times to go and eat by the harbour. Out of insistence rather than genuine attraction, they ended up an item. Maggie went with him to his shows. She sat near the stage and drank beer. She was living a new life within her old one. She understood that Brailovsky was the impromptu protagonist of a fantasy.

★

The Russian survived on a wartime economy. He scraped through with his live shows and some private lessons. He'd never moved out of his parents' home. In Chapadmalal, fittingly, he'd had his baptism by fire at the age of eighteen. It was a January afternoon. Thanks to a friend, Brailovsky was working as a pot washer in a buffet restaurant. His hands were all cracked and his nails were cloudy. Back then, in the early evening of every working day, he'd step out to the back yard to smoke a Chesterfield under the shade of an elm tree. That was his truce. He'd stay still, frozen but not absent. The cigarette, from hand to mouth, mouth to hand. Once, a blonde guy stepped out of the pool and hit him by mistake with his towel. The Russian pretended not to notice, he was unwilling to react. Two seconds later, the guy spat out an insult. Brailovsky straightened up, widened his stance and offered his face. There was a prologue: two shoves. Right after, the confusion of the fight: some grappling and then a scratch. In the struggle, Brailovsky lost his balance and fell against a protruding wall: his chin split in half. It was a minor wound but it left him with a scar, a horseshoe with blunt edges. It was this mark that, years later, determined the pattern that led Maggie, a woman driven by sudden impulses, to leave him abruptly. The stamp left by that fight was a line, a meaningless drawing, but its location on his face – a veritable theatre – betrayed the truth that his expressions concealed.

★

After lunch, Maggie ate a tangerine. She had picked a café on Playa Grande for the final encounter. She got there at 2.30 p.m. and took a table by the window. She realised straight away: she was in the wrong place. The main area – a room painted in Hare Krishna orange – was more like a kitchen, or rather, the kitchen in a run-down house. It was a café with high ceilings and a wooden counter behind which, on the wall, there was a Junghans station-style clock and three shelves with bottles of whisky, aperitifs and liqueurs.

The Russian was on time. He was carrying his guitar case in one hand and said he'd just come from doing an interview. He was parched. Lowering his gaze, he ran his tongue over his lips and ordered a tonic water. A small bottle of Schweppes, ice cold, he said to the waiter. The guy shook his head and glanced at Maggie. With a gesture, Brailovsky minimised the significance of the matter. He went for another brand although, deep down, he regretted the lack of Schweppes. He read this as an indicator of the state of things. Disconcerted by the unexpected sense of threat, he talked non-stop. She seemed distracted.

When the waiter brought the bottle to the table, Brailovsky fell silent and Maggie went for it. I don't love you and I am not attracted to you, she said. At that moment, a lorry went by with a broken exhaust. I don't love you and I am not attracted to you, she repeated. Brailovsky endured stoically. Maggie's words took him by surprise, but the composure with which he bore them did so far more. After ten seconds, he let out a groan. There was nothing to say. They remained in silence until they gathered energy to leave. They parted ways with barely a word. The sea was grey and turbid. The waves were hardly moving, but the crests vibrated. That afternoon, two dispositions were merging in the water.

When she got to the flat on Calle Camusso, Maggie closed the window and threw herself onto the bed fully dressed. She didn't even take her boots off. There was an impression fluttering in her mind that made her think that, despite it all, things were turning out all right for her. The world, as arbitrary as a spinning top, was succumbing to her wishes. She took a deep breath and squinted. It was 3.15 p.m. The siesta hour was making its presence felt. Nothing in the air, nothing at all, gave the slightest indication that in less than seven minutes the boiler of the Materia soap factory would explode, and that the atmosphere in the neighbourhood, so bright and composed at that moment, would fill with chaos, dust and a whitish residue that, bit by bit, would settle over things, heavy like snow. Snow as hushed and unyielding as destiny itself.

ACKNOWLEDGEMENTS

I want to thank Miguel Vitagliano, Aníbal Jarkowski, Natalia Viñes, Liliana Herrero, Hernán Ronsino, Christian Kupchik, Oliverio Coelho, Ricardo Romero, Gustavo Ferreyra, Pablo Braun, Leonora Djament and, of course, the *chochis* Natalia and Luciana, for the shared conversations, the readings and the wealth of ideas.

I also want to thank Carolina Orloff in particular, for her lucid, careful and loving way of looking.

CHARCO PRESS

Director & Editor: Carolina Orloff
Director: Samuel McDowell

www.charcopress.com

Southerly was published on
90gsm Munken Premium Cream paper.

The text was designed using Bembo 11.5 and ITC Galliard.

Printed in January 2023 by TJ Books
Padstow, Cornwall, PL28 8RW using responsibly
sourced paper and environmentally-friendly adhesive.

MIX
Paper from
responsible sources
FSC® C013056